Cover Design: Missy Walker

Editor: Swish Design & Editing

To Dad,
I miss you so much. I wish you were here to see what I'm
accomplishing—though, let's be honest, I hope you'd
never actually read my books! You were always my
biggest champion.

BROKEN RULES

ELITE MEN OF LOS ANGELES #2

MISSY WALKER

1

───────

LEX

When I was a kid, I used to have nightmares about showing up at school in my underwear and being called up to deliver a report I hadn't written. More than once, I dreamed I was the star of the school play, but I had never gone to a rehearsal. It was opening night, and all eyes were on me—unprepared, deer-in-headlights me.

This was no nightmare, though it felt like one. I was standing in my father's office, which, at times, had felt more like home to me as a kid than the house I grew up in. The studio was on the brink of producing my first major film, a project Dad was counting on essentially turning around the studio's lackluster numbers. Imagine my surprise to find out he went behind my back and secured a notoriously difficult director without my input. As if it wasn't bad enough, he had chosen the script without me and was already reaching out to agents to secure the actors *he* wanted.

Now, I was faced with the last person I would ever have hired for this or any project. Summer Strawbridge, with her shitty attitude and insistence that she always knew what was best and her artistic vision couldn't possibly falter. Word traveled fast around here, and everybody knew that certain people who weren't worth the pain in the ass they might deliver.

It didn't seem to matter since she was standing in front of me, giving me the up and down like I was a slug, and she was deciding whether to squash me or let me go on my way. She looked like she had just left some artist commune with the boho outfit she'd thrown together. And yet, somehow, she managed to look down on me?

"I know we're all looking forward to getting started." Dad was either unaware of the sudden tension in the air or didn't care. I'd go with the latter because why would he? As far as he was concerned, she was my problem. He'd expect the same results regardless —a film with the power to breathe new life into the Landry International brand.

"I know I am," she chirped. Did she realize how everything about her changed when she turned away from me to face him? That withering expression she wore a split second ago turned to something brighter and hopeful—just an eager girl looking to prove herself.

Had she ever considered acting as a profession? If she had, I could see why she had given it up in favor of directing because she was no good at pretending she wasn't desperate as hell. Her smile was too hard, almost brittle, much like the light shining from her eyes with determination and mania. I could respect one. I wasn't sure I wanted to work with the other.

Not that I had a choice because, as usual, Dad had gone over my head and done exactly what he wanted and now expected me to play nice and accept his word as law. I'd ask myself where he got off, but I knew the answer. He had always gotten away with it. Why would that stop now?

"And do you understand we are looking at a rushed schedule?" Dad asked, watching her closely. "I wasn't sure if word had gotten to you yet."

If she hadn't already rubbed me the wrong way, looking at me the way she did, I might have felt sorry for her. She didn't know she was being tested. The girl had only walked in moments ago wearing her loose, flowing dress and arms full of bangles, the sort of look that gave me the impression of an artistic, free spirit type. In other words, was she going to adhere to a rigid schedule, or was she somebody who relied on her horoscope to make decisions for her?

Her smile slipped, but not by much. "A rushed schedule?" she asked. I couldn't read her expression but imagined her panicking inside.

"Yes, we had a scheduling conflict and had to shift projects around to accommodate. Lex will tell you all about it," he offered, throwing my ass under the bus. "This is his baby. I have to remind myself to keep my hands out of it." With an indulgent laugh, two out of three of us knew he didn't mean, he looked my way. "Son, I'm handing the reins over to you. I would invite the two of you to talk it over here, in my office, but I have a meeting in a few minutes."

The bastard.

The motherfucker.

Putting me on the spot this way, saddling me with her, and then stepping back and playing innocent. It was part of the new persona he was trying to put together in his old age—the benevolent, grandfatherly figure. I didn't care for it.

But it was the hand I'd been dealt, and a pair of clear, green eyes watched my every move. I had to rise to the occasion before she got the idea I didn't know what I was doing.

"Let me lead you to my office, Miss Strawbridge." I was out to sea, flailing blindly, but I'd be damned if I gave any hint of that as I opened the door to my father's office and stepped aside so she could pass.

I realized as I led the way to the office cattycorner from my father's, on the opposite end of the floor, that we had something in common. We were both a little shell-shocked. "There's a small, unused office here," I pointed out, opening the door to the room next to my office. "You're free to take it for the duration of the project." She looked around, not saying a word, her stiff body language screaming a single word. *Rage.*

It was obvious she hadn't been given all of the details, the same as me. It might have brought us closer, given us something to bond over. Should I clear the air and laugh over this?

She made up my mind for me as we entered the

room, one considerably smaller than the one we had left. I had only started putting my own touches on it. Truth be told, with Dad considering retirement, part of me wanted to wait until I moved into his office before settling in.

Turning to me as soon as we were alone, she folded her arms. Gone was the sunny, almost painfully sincere and driven girl Dad met. I was looking at the real Summer, whose chin jutted out when she was pissed off. "Is this your policy?"

"Meaning what?" And why the fuck was she so combative straight off the bat? We had barely exchanged a few sentences, yet the woman glared at me like I had personally destroyed her life.

"Meaning, I wasn't told anything about a rushed schedule when I agreed to do this picture. How rushed are we talking?"

"Six months to the premiere," I announced. Why bother easing into it? She wanted to play tough, so I'd give her what she wanted. "You're welcome to tell us to fuck ourselves if you don't think that's possible. Better to get it out of the way now."

Her head snapped back like she'd been struck, and her eyes widened a fraction. For the first time, we were on equal footing, both of us flailing to make sense of what we'd been thrown into. We were both trapped since she had to know we were the only studio in town willing to hire her. There was no choice but to comply if she wanted to work.

The illusion of solidarity didn't last long. "Now I see why you wanted me for this," she announced, jutting a hip out to the side, still staring me down in my office. "I can't imagine any other director capable of getting the job done in such a ridiculously short amount of time. Why did we bother having this meeting? I should be out scouting locations as we speak."

I shouldn't have bristled at her strident, almost overly confident tone of voice. Cocky, even. "There are procedures we need to follow first, you realize." Taking a seat at my desk, I gestured for her to do the same in one of the leather chairs on the opposite side. She hesitated, lips pursed, but gave in before long. Why did everything have to be a contest with her?

"How many movies have you produced, Mr. Landry?" She took a seat, moving gracefully, crossing her legs under her long, linen dress. Something unexpected stirred in me as I watched closer than I should have. I couldn't help it. It was hardwired in me. When I saw a beautiful woman, I reacted. It was nature.

And I couldn't deny she was beautiful, or she might have been if she put a little effort into herself. She was barefaced. Her auburn hair looked like she might have run her fingers through it before putting it up in a sloppy bun. The ugly sandals she wore were so old they were practically gasping for air, barely clinging to life. I didn't think it was my imagination, the faint aroma of incense following her around. It reminded me of when I saw her at my father's honorary industry event, where her version of 'dressing up' looked more like a protest against nice clothes.

This wannabe hippie was going to question me? "This will be the first film my name is on," I admitted since there was nothing to be ashamed of. "But rest assured, I grew up behind the studio gates. I felt more at home here than I did anywhere else." What did I think I would get admitting that? A little understanding? The hope she might soften?

I was disappointed. "But you've never produced a major film?"

A fucking Google search could've told her that. Dammit, she knew how to hit a nerve. "I know exactly what needs to be done." Where the fuck did she get off, anyway?

"Good, because we're in a hurry." She reached into the tasseled satchel bag she carried over her shoulder and pulled out a thick binder, which she opened on her lap. "I have all of this information on my MacBook, as well, and I can forward it to you."

"What information would that be?"

"I've put together a list of actors who are perfect for this. People who immediately came to mind when I read the script." It was almost cute how naïve she was. I almost hated bursting her bubble.

Almost.

Because she had started us off on the wrong foot, glaring at me like I didn't deserve to breathe air. "That's very nice, and I'm sure it will be taken into consideration."

She looked up from the pages she flipped through, arching an eyebrow. "You aren't interested in seeing the list?"

I folded my hands on my desk the way I'd seen Dad do countless times. "Miss Strawbridge, let's get something straight."

"Summer."

"Pardon me?"

"My name is Summer. You don't need to call me

Miss Strawbridge. You're not old enough to put on the whole formal act."

This arrogant little bitch. She had a point, but how she delivered it left me biting back a growl. "I hope you don't think that means you get to call me Lex."

"I wouldn't make an assumption like that."

"Thank you. Sum*mer*," I continued, emphasizing her name, "I understand what you must be dealing with right now. You're still fairly untested, new in town."

She bristled. "Not exactly new."

Why was everything an argument? "You were in talks to helm two different films at other studios," I snapped. "And both times, you were replaced by other, more experienced directors. What would you call that?"

"I've directed five independent features, one of which premiered at Cannes and won the award for Best Short Film."

"That was Eric Danvers' film," I reminded her. The director I wanted. His work on *Road to Glory* proved he was a master at capturing breakneck speed on film. I almost forgot to breathe more than once during the climactic race scene with its daring camera angles that fully immersed me in the action. He would've been perfect for another longer feature revolving around a group of amateur race car drivers.

"It's a long story." Her posture went rigid, like someone stuck a broomstick down the back of her dress. "Rest assured, my fingerprints are all over the finished product, regardless of whether my name appears in the credits."

Interesting. It wouldn't be the first example of someone being cut out of a finished product after pouring themselves into it. For every star on the Walk of Fame, there were hundreds of stories of people whose dreams were shattered.

"What happened?" I asked. "Was there some kind of falling out?"

Somehow, she managed to go even stiffer. "That's personal."

"I'm asking for the sake of understanding what I'm getting into with you. Was there a creative disagreement with Eric Danvers?"

"Yes." Her jaw tightened, and a sneer curled her lip. "There was a disagreement. A falling out. And he decided to pretend I didn't carry that entire film on my back. And because he's a man, everyone believed him that I was impossible. Difficult. Stubborn. A bitch," she concluded, the word exploding from her mouth.

"Are you?" What was wrong with me? Why the hell did I ask her that? It had to be the attitude she carried. There was a wall of energy around her, hot and prickly. Something about it touched a perverse part of me that wanted to antagonize her, and I didn't know why.

"Do you expect me to say yes?" she countered. "Would that make it easier for you if I said yes, I'm a real bitch when I put my mind to it? Exactly how would you define a bitch?"

This was a mistake. I held up my hands in mock surrender, chuckling. "Fine. You don't need to twist my balls. It was a joke."

"Was it? I thought jokes were supposed to be funny."

How did I define a bitch? For starters, I was looking at one. "And I thought a newcomer to the industry being given a huge opportunity with a major studio was supposed to be grateful instead of combative."

"Who said I'm not grateful? I know this is a great opportunity." She stood in one quick, graceful movement, slinging her satchel over one slim shoulder and resting the binder on her hip. "That doesn't mean I'm going to bow and scrape. If that's what you're looking for, Mr. Landry, you've got the wrong girl. Thank you for wasting my time."

She was going to leave. She actually started for the door, sandals slapping the floor, muttering something under her breath. I was torn between wanting to see how far she would go and being distracted by her perfect peach of an ass as it swayed under the loose, linen dress.

Finally, my good sense won out, and I found my voice. "You've made your point."

She stopped but kept her back to me. "What point do you think I'm trying to make?" she asked in an icy tone.

"Have you forgotten you're talking to the executive producer of the film you're trying to direct?"

"Have you forgotten you're not going to have a film without a director?" She slowly pivoted on her heel, revealing a smirk. "I understand word got around about me. But it's gotten around about you too. And I know you wanted Eric on this. We still have plenty of mutual friends."

Dammit. How was I supposed to know they were connected somehow? Irritation set my teeth on edge. I didn't appreciate her smug expression, the humor in it, and the feeling of being exposed.

"I quoted a couple of potential directors," I

allowed, fighting to stay calm when I wanted more than anything to throw her out of my office on her ass. No wonder she couldn't break into this town. Nobody wanted her, myself included, but then I didn't have much choice.

"But it was your father's people who reached out to me and worked out the terms. Not you. Why is that?" she asked, feigning innocence while a nasty smirk played across her lips.

Gritting my teeth, I stood. "Let's get one thing straight, Strawbridge."

"I thought you were going to call me Summer."

"Summer," I spat before I could stop myself. "If you don't want this job, be my guest and let me know now. There's still time to find somebody else."

"You aren't going to find anybody capable of doing a better job with this script than I can and definitely not in six months. I already have the entire film in my head." She tapped two fingers to her temple. "I understand these characters... their emotion and turmoil. Nobody can put that on the screen the way I can."

Where had this side of her been hiding? This burning, passionate intensity? She didn't need to shout, wave her arms, or make demands to get her point across.

"I'd like to hear some of your thoughts on the script," I offered, struggling to soften my approach. "It might be nice to get an idea of what you're envisioning." Because at the end of the day, she'd signed a contract and was attached to the project. I had no idea how long it would take to find a worthy director with such short notice.

Tipping her head to the side, she retorted, "We could have been doing that all this time if you hadn't wasted this meeting by turning it into a pissing contest."

Was that what I had been doing? Everything in me reared up in denial. Who gave her the right to talk to me that way? And how the hell did she have the balls to call me out? Because that was exactly what I had done. It had been a pissing contest since the moment we set eyes on each other.

But she had set the tone. Not me. Would I accuse her of that? No, even if it was true. One of us had to be the bigger person if there was any hope of making this work. "Fine. Why don't we start over? There's a lot of work to get through and very little time to get it done."

"Unfortunately," she replied with a sigh. "A lot of that work involves doing something other than sitting in an office. I have locations to scout, and it looks like I'll need to revise the entire shooting schedule to accommodate the timeline. We'll have to touch base again tomorrow."

Turning toward the door, she added, "I'm looking forward to it."

I would've stopped her, but I couldn't string two words together.

How the fuck was I supposed to survive six months with this woman?

2

SUMMER

"**M**otherfucker! Stupid asshole!" I gripped the pillow tighter, pressing it to my face and screaming again. "You fucking bastard!"

Usually, screaming like this helped me release whatever was weighing me down or burning inside me. Sadly, it seemed there was no getting rid of what was burning in my chest by the time I reached the cheap motel room I was renting until the studio set me up with an apartment as per our contract.

The fucking contract where I was supposed to have a year until release. *Not six months*. I slammed the pillow against the bed a few times, relishing the way my shoulders ached from the effort. But it still wasn't enough. I wanted blood. Specifically, the blood of Lex Landry.

To go with the blood of so many others who'd fucked me over from day one.

"You finished?" Claudia turned away from the tea kettle on the stove, crossing from the tiny kitchenette to where I sat on one of the two double beds. My best friend knew well enough to stay out of my way when I was raging. Now, she brought me a cup of chamomile tea in hopes of soothing whatever was left.

There wasn't tea in the state of California to do that, but I groaned and accepted the mug. "You don't understand. He was such a prick. Strutting around the place, and why? Because he was the swimmer that reached his mother's egg first? Congratulations, Lex Landry. You were born wealthy." Even the honey Claudia had added to the tea tasted sour in my mouth.

"You knew what you were getting into," she reminded me, took a seat on the other bed and tucked her black curls behind her ear. We were close enough that our knees nearly touched as we sipped from our mugs. "This is a major studio. They're not interested in art."

"I didn't know what I was getting into," I countered as indignation flared in my chest again. "I thought I was working with Alexander. The father. The one who actually has a fucking clue. But no, I get pushed off on the idiot nepo baby who's been coasting on his last name his entire life. That goes to show you how much respect they have for me."

"It doesn't have to be a respect thing," she pointed out gently.

"What is it?" I asked. "I know what everybody thinks about me. I know they figure I'm too much trouble to deal with, so why bother?"

"Word does get around," she murmured, biting her lip as she always did when she was anxious. It took a lot to shake her, and that's probably why we had become instant friends on the first day of first grade. We had balanced each other out for almost twenty-five years. Now, she was my assistant since she was better with people and scheduling than I could ever hope to be.

"What is that supposed to mean?" I asked. "Don't do that. Don't sound like them."

"I don't mean to. Let's face it. You need this."

If there was one thing I hated more than just about anything else besides arrogant nepo babies who only cared about money, it was being called out. "It's not my fault," I whispered.

Right away, she winced, reaching out to pat my leg. "You know I didn't mean it that way. It's not your fault your boyfriend was the king of slimy shits and left you to navigate the world of pervy producers and studio heads."

I set the mug down on the table between our beds, flopped onto my back and stared up at the ceiling with its stained tiles. Two years. It had been two years since I had been stabbed in the back, and there were days like today when the pain was as fresh as ever.

His voice echoed in my memory, dripping with false sincerity the way it had when he broke the news that I was excluded from the film's credits. *"It was an oversight. That's how these things go sometimes. No hard feelings."* It wasn't bad enough the bastard broke my heart when he stuck his dick in another woman, he had to crush me professionally too. He had to burn every last bridge that connected us.

Even that hadn't been enough. He also had to cover his ass to make sure his version of events got out before I could set the record straight. He wouldn't want everyone to know I had carried that fucking movie for the better part of a year. I had worked tirelessly while he battled his so-called demons, sometimes holing up for days on end in a drunken stupor while I handled rewrites, rescheduling, and reshoots. I had sat with the editors and cobbled together the finished product that ended up sending my ex to Cannes.

A finished product that only bore the name Eric Danvers.

"She's difficult. She's demanding. It's her way or no way." I could hear the words coming out of his mouth if I tried hard enough. I could hear how he sounded. How condescending he was. The poor, put-upon man forced to work with a woman who had standards and boundaries.

"Of course," I whispered. "Everybody believes the man."

"If you try to defend yourself, you look like the screaming harpy," Claudia concluded. Then, all of a sudden, she jumped up, startling me into lifting my head to watch her.

"What are you doing?" I asked.

"I'm going to make you a sage bundle to burn in Landry's office the next time you're there."

She was probably serious, but the idea made me laugh anyway. "I don't know if there's enough sage in your collection to handle all that shitty energy," I mused.

"It's still worth trying. Anyway, whether you want

to be or not, you're on the hook for this movie. And I know you're going to make it good." She looked over her shoulder from where she stood at the chipped dresser, going through her stash of herbs and flowers. Her dark eyes crinkled at the corners when she grinned. "We both know you are. And we both know you can work through adversity."

Yes, that much I knew from personal experience. "Is it always going to feel like an uphill battle?"

"Hopefully, no. But that depends on you, too, and you know it."

"Ugh…" I groaned as my head dropped to the bed again. "Remind me why I asked you to be my assistant."

"Because I love you." Looking over her shoulder again, she added, "And I'm the only person who'll put up with you."

"I should bring you with me to my next meeting with that dickhead." I didn't want to say his name. It left a bad taste in my mouth.

"Don't threaten me with a good time." When I barked out a laugh, she shrugged. "I'm serious. I can't wait to meet him."

"Gross," I groaned out, crossing my arms over my eyes.

"Listen. I know Fuck Face Eric burned you big

time, and I wouldn't blame you if you swore off men for the rest of your life. But don't act like you can't see how hot Lex Landry is. Remember those photos from that awards thing they threw for his dad? Whew." She fanned herself, going back to the sage bundle.

"I might throw up."

"That's right, keep pretending," she murmured as she worked. "The more you fight, the more I know I'm right."

Objectively, the man was handsome. Hot. Tall, broad shoulders, with a killer body and a head full of thick, luscious brown hair. He had the sort of soulful, dark eyes that seemed able to bore holes through me, a jawline sharp enough to cut glass, and a mouth that could only be described as sensuous.

It was a real shame he had to be an arrogant dickhead.

"You forget, I've already ignored a hundred red flags because a guy was hot," I whispered, letting my arms fall away from my face. "All his bullshit. All his pandering to me. He tricked me into believing he actually cared about art and integrity."

"Not everybody is Eric." The bedsprings creaked when Claudia sat next to me. There was no more humor in her voice. She wasn't teasing anymore.

"You can't carry all that old shit into this project. It's going to ruin everything, and you deserve better than that. Don't sabotage yourself."

"Like I do it on purpose," I mumbled.

"That's not what I said. Just keep it in mind."

When my phone rang, there was a split second when I wondered if it was Lex Landry calling. It turned out that part of me still wanted to cling to childish fantasies. I wanted to believe he might call and apologize for starting on the wrong foot and throwing my so-called reputation in my face.

I would have to grow up at some point. "Shit," I whispered, my heart sinking when I saw it was Mom calling me. "I have to play happy now."

"Tell her I said hi." Claudia ducked into the small bathroom and closed the door. I decided to step outside rather than have the conversation in the room. I needed some fresh air.

I answered on my way out the door, injecting sunshine into my voice. "Hi. How's it going?"

Mom's laughter rang out. "Don't be silly. You know why I'm calling. How was your meeting at the studio?"

"It was great," I lied, squeezing my eyes shut. Thirty years old and still wincing when I told my mother a lie.

"Really?" She sounded skeptical, to say the least. "Everything went well?"

"Just as well as it could. As it turns out, Lex Landry is executive producing. The son of the studio head."

"That's great news!"

"Why do you say that?" I asked with a disbelieving laugh. If there was one thing my parents didn't care about, it was Hollywood in general. The fact that she sounded positive in the first place shocked the shit out of me. There was one thing I had been raised to resent, and it was the sort of people who made millions from the artistic endeavors of other people who had to jump from job to job, trying to cobble together a livelihood. They were the true artists, the people putting their blood, sweat, and tears into their work.

"If he's younger and untested, you can take control. You can make sure your vision is honored, Summer. This could be the ultimate opportunity for you. Working with someone who isn't set in his ways."

There were a few things I appreciated more than my mother's positivity. I was used to hearing her look at the bright side of things no matter how dark the situation seemed. Right now, though, I wasn't in the mood to be cheered up. I was still wallowing. Immature? I knew it was. All the knowledge made me do was dig my heels in deeper, determined to sulk because I knew I shouldn't.

"I'm sure you're right," I lied again, pacing the walkway near the hotel parking lot.

"Have you found an apartment yet?"

"No. There's something in my contract about them finding one for me. I forgot to bring it up at the meeting." There were a lot of things I forgot to bring up at the meeting. Why the hell did I walk out? My heart sank as my back hit the brick wall. I slid down it until I was crouched with my knees close to my chest. What was I thinking? I needed to get out of this damn motel and move somewhere I could spread out a little—somewhere to unpack instead of living out of my suitcases.

There was just something about Lex Landry that got under my skin. It wasn't a great excuse, but it was the truth.

"I hope it's soon. I would love to come out and take a look at it."

"Yeah, that'll be fun." And that made three lies in less than two minutes. Not that I didn't want to see them, but there was a reason I preferred visiting Mom and Dad rather than having them come out to see me. It was never long before they had to share their opinions on everything from filmmakers selling their talents to the highest bidder like high-priced whores to actors and actresses who'd rather sacrifice themselves on the altar of fame than nurture their creative fire in so-called legitimate theater.

As far as they were concerned, nobody was a true artist unless they were suffering somehow. People who made art for money were sellouts, a belief that had been drilled into their heads from the time their parents migrated to San Francisco back in the free-love days.

I had figured it out at a young age, watching Mom fight to sell her pottery and Dad obsess over his latest mixed-media installation which not many people ever cared about. Their failures had only hardened their opinion, which said more about their lack of success than it did about anything else. Why be happy for the success of others when resentment was more immediate and soothing?

After a while, it had become a matter of sunk cost fallacy until the demands of three growing daughters meant tucking their tails between their legs and moving to an actual neighborhood with dependable utilities and trash pickup.

"Don't worry," she added. "If things don't go well this time around, remember what we told you. You can always come home. Your room is ready for you. Though I'd have to get my pottery supplies out of there," she murmured, almost as an afterthought to herself.

Staring across the parking lot and the horizon beyond it, my resolve hardened in the rays of the early afternoon sun. *Like hell.* There weren't many things that chilled my blood like the thought of moving back home did. I had sort of gotten used to the idea of living somewhere with air conditioning, a garbage disposal, not to mention more than one bathroom so I wouldn't have to share it with my damn parents. No matter how many times I tried to remind them that an artist didn't have to live like a pauper to be legitimate, they didn't want to hear it. That was their choice.

Not mine.

But that didn't make me like Lex Landry, either. I was nothing like him or the people who inhabited his world.

"I'm sure it's going to work out just fine," I said. Was that a lie? Not if I believed it, which I had to. I knew what this film needed, and it was me as its director. If Lex only cared about dollars and cents and getting this finished by the impossible deadline, that was fine. It meant I'd have to work harder and smarter to keep the film's integrity in one piece.

"That's my girl. But the offer always stands," she reminded me. "Sometimes I wish you had chosen something a little less cutthroat. If you wanted to direct, there was that position with the local children's theater—"

"I'm sorry, I'd better go," I murmured, cutting her off so I wouldn't throw up if I heard her talk about that damn children's theater director position one more time. Running two-week theater camps for school kids was nothing like directing a major motion picture.

"Just keep us posted, okay? Your sisters have been asking about you too. You should reach out to them."

"I will." Even if I had no desire to talk about Aura's beekeeping hobby or Rainbow's latest rescue dog, I loved my sisters, I loved my family, but I was always different—more driven and less inclined to walk barefoot through my garden on the way to the beehives or whatever it was Aura kept in her backyard.

"Tell Claudia we send our love," Mom added, and I promised to as we ended the call.

I sighed, staring longingly toward the Hollywood Hills in the distance. It had taken a long time for me to come to grips with the idea there was nothing wrong with wanting to be part of that existence. To have a career in Hollywood, to make the sort of movies people would see instead of the kind that got buried for lack of a promotions department behind them. I wanted to sit at the table with the men who had ruled the town and industry for much too long. I wanted to make my mark.

If only that didn't mean having to jump in the mud with these pigs and splash around, fighting for dominance.

But I would if it meant I'd finally win.

Even if Lex Landry insisted on getting in the way.

3

LEX

"Somehow, I have to find a way to make this work," I concluded, then bolted back the rest of my whiskey. It didn't do much to ease the resentment that had raged in me ever since I set eyes on Summer Strawbridge earlier.

I hadn't been able to get her out of my head, no matter how I tried, and I did since the last thing I wanted was to spend my entire day focused on her. I had calls to make, meetings to schedule, permits to obtain. I would need Summer's list of shooting locations, to say nothing of the whirlwind casting process.

For once, my friends didn't smirk or bust my balls when I was finished. It was something we made a habit of—the four of us—never taking ourselves or each other too seriously. There were times when they were all that kept me grounded since it was pretty easy in Hollywood to start listening to your own publicity. Good, honest friends like the ones I had managed to find over the years to keep me from making that mistake.

"That fucking sucks." Travis Knight only shrugged and shook his head. "I wish there was something more to say, really."

"You have to do it all in six months?" Clayton Manning raised a skeptical eyebrow. "I don't know anything about the process, but that seems like a tight timeline even to me. I could never open a new restaurant in six months."

"It's fucking impossible," I blurted out, rubbing my temples. "But the whole fucking future of the studio could hang on this. We need something to turn it around."

"You know, the same shit is going on in so many industries." Spencer Collins signaled a passing server for more drinks. Her warm, inviting smile was lost on him. He had lived with his girlfriend, Rowan, for the past month after they'd reconnected, and in the process, he had discovered a ten-year-old daughter he never knew he had. The days of him getting his dick wet with some random server were long gone.

"What do you mean?" I asked.

"Well, look at my cousin, Connor," he explained. "Diamond Media is the biggest out there, but they still had to pivot into digital media when print started declining. Other media brands either couldn't or wouldn't change their approach, and he wound up buying them out when they failed. You have to be willing to change with the times."

"The times are changing," I growled out. "And I get to clean up the mess."

"You could say no," Travis pointed out. He was normally the smartass of the group, but now he was serious. "You don't need to work for the studio. Do your own thing. You have the money, you have connections."

He was speaking from experience, having built his own shipping business after interning with Spencer's father years ago. That was where he and Spencer met when their fathers sent them overseas to learn the ropes. Rather than come home and work for his dad, Travis had decided to strike out on his own. Now, he sat at the head of what was rapidly becoming an empire, snowballing faster than even he had ever hoped while somehow raising a kid on his own.

He had a point. Walking away was an option. I had more than enough money to my name, enough to start a studio of my own if I wanted to. But my father's face floated in front of my mind's eye, and I wiped that idea away like a marker off a dry-erase board. "I'm not going to walk away," I decided. "I refuse to let him think I can't hack it."

"There's only one solution, then." Leaning back in his chair, Clay crossed one ankle over the other knee. "You'll have to fuck this Summer Strawbridge until she's too exhausted and sore to put up a fight."

They burst out into predictable laughter, though I didn't join them. "Please," I protested. "Her pussy probably has teeth."

"Ouch." Travis winced and made a show of grabbing his crotch, laughing as our fresh drinks arrived. He eyed the server like she was dessert, staring at her tits, eyes glued when she turned away. "Goddamn, that is a glorious ass."

"You said she's some artsy, hippie type?" Clay questioned, and I rolled my eyes, starting in on my second drink. "You never know. She could be one of those yoga chicks. Super flexible."

"That must be how she manages to wedge her

head up her ass," I muttered, making them laugh again. They didn't get it. They hadn't met her.

"She's still a woman," Spencer insisted. "I've seen you melt the panties off a woman at fifty yards. All you have to do is smile."

"It's not like that," I insisted. "She walked in with a chip on her shoulder. The second she set eyes on me, she made up her mind."

"The way you did?" Spencer cocked an eyebrow.

That was all it took for the fire in my chest to explode into an inferno. "Do me a favor," I snapped. "Don't treat me like your kid. Just because you're getting laid on the regular doesn't mean you're an expert all of a sudden."

"Fuck off." He laughed. "I'm sorry if the truth hurts, buddy."

"I've got shit to do." I tossed cash on the table, downing the rest of my drink and slamming the glass back into place. "Good to see you."

"Come on," Clay urged. "Don't be like that."

It was too late. I was too frustrated and bitter, and the fact that nobody seemed to understand only made it worse. They weren't there. They hadn't locked eyes with that woman and realized she was unreachable.

It only hit me once I was behind the wheel of my

Maserati that I didn't feel like going home. It was too early to go home alone, for one thing, but then I didn't feel like going anywhere to find someone to help me pass a few hours. I wasn't in the mood. I wouldn't be good company, either. Granted, there were women who didn't give a shit about the company so long as the man they were with had enough room on his credit card, but I wasn't interested in that. Maybe in my younger days, fresh out of school, when I walked around with a perpetual hard-on.

Now, I was the presumed heir to a movie studio. I had an image to uphold.

It seemed like my body had a mind of its own because before I knew it, I was rolling through the gates to Landry International. The studio was quiet, the windows to the offices darkened. A security guard rolled past in a golf cart and lifted a hand, a gesture I returned, pulling into my reserved spot. It wasn't only Summer I couldn't get out of my head but the movie itself. The work that had to be done. I had left my laptop in my office and decided now to take it home. If I wasn't going to spend the night screwing around, I might as well be productive.

Apparently, I wasn't the only one with that idea. The small room next to my office was in use, light pouring out from under the closed door. The noise coming from behind the door set the hair at the back of my neck on end. An intruder? What the hell would they be doing in an unused office? They should be in mine or Dad's.

I marched toward the door, only realizing as I was turning the knob that there could be someone with a weapon on the other side. Too late. I threw the door open, prepared to lay into whoever thought they could sneak around here after hours.

Summer's sharp gasp pierced the air. She stood bolt upright beside a large metal desk that now sat in the center of the room. She was flushed, breathless, and her face fell when she noted my presence. "Oh. It's you. You told me I could have this as my office."

"How did you think you were going to move this yourself?" I asked, walking over to the opposite end of the desk while she brushed strands of sweat-dampened hair away from her face. "Where do you want it?"

"There." She pointed to a space in front of the room's only window, which overlooked the parking lot.

"Right. On my count." I took firm hold of the desk, and she scrambled to do the same. "One, two, three." The fucker was heavy. How long had she been trying to inch it across the floor by herself?

"Thank you," she groaned out once it was in place, wheeling an old office chair behind it and dropping like a rock. "Honestly, I thought I'd never get the thing moved."

"Do you always have to do everything by yourself?"

"Lately? Yes," she replied, sighing. "My assistant was going to come over and help me, but she had a family thing to take care of. Her parents live in the Valley," she explained, running her tanned arm over her forehead to catch the perspiration on her skin.

"Oh. Well, glad I showed up at the right moment." How awkward was this?

"Why did you come back?" she asked, her brows pinching in confusion.

I had to laugh as I crossed the room, ready to get the hell out of there while we were still getting along. What was it about her that made me so uneasy, unsettled? I only knew I didn't like it. "A studio boss' work is never done."

"But you're not the boss, are you?" she pointed out. The girl might as well have fired an arrow into my back or a bullet with the power to tear through the goodwill I was trying to foster.

"What is it with you?" I demanded, spinning on my heel in time to watch her mouth fall open. Did she think she could get away with being a smartass indefinitely? That I'd never call her on it? "What's with the antagonistic attitude?"

"I was joking."

If anything, the innocent act deepened my rage, heating my blood. "The minute you knew you'd be working with me and not my father, your whole attitude shifted," I snapped. "I watched it happen, so don't pretend I don't know what I'm talking about. What did I do to deserve that? I wanted to start off on the right foot."

"So did I." For the first time, there was no argument in her voice. It was soft now, almost regretful. "I didn't mean to start things off that way. But wouldn't you be pissed off if you found out there was a bait-and-switch going on? Nobody told me I'd be working with you and not your dad. How would you feel if that was dropped in your lap with no warning?"

"Pretty much the same way I'd feel if a director I wasn't expecting to work with was dropped in my lap at the last moment," I admitted, sighing. "We both need this. I wouldn't normally spill my guts, but it's the truth, and you deserve to know it."

She was wary, her eyes narrowed as they looked me up and down. "What do you mean, we both need it? Is this your dad's way of testing you?"

"What makes you say that?"

"It's your first movie," she reminded me with a smirk. "He wants to see if you can pull it off. You have to prove yourself."

My spine stiffened. "I don't have to prove myself to anyone."

Her smirk deepened into a grin. "But you want to."

"It would be nice," I admitted.

"It would be nice to have your problems. I don't have the luxury of messing up. I have to prove myself because I'm a woman."

I was almost too late to stop myself from rolling my eyes. The past few years, I'd been bombarded with stories of how difficult it was for a woman to make it in Hollywood, no matter what career she pursued. I didn't doubt it, but the song was starting to get a little old after playing on repeat. "It's more than that, and we both know it," I reminded her. "You have a reputation. If we're clearing the air, let's clear it for good."

She bristled, and I regretted it, but it was too late to take it back. "Exactly what have you heard about me? Tell me the truth," she added, like a threat. Like there was anything she could do to retaliate if I lied.

"I heard you're difficult. I've seen that much for myself." She rolled her eyes, but I continued, "You're stubborn. You refuse to compromise. When Clyde Harris over at Sunset Pictures asked you to take on an assistant director, you quit the fucking movie. Tell me I'm wrong."

"You know, that is hilarious," she hissed as color flooded her cheeks. "You honestly believe I'd quit a movie at Sunset because I had to work with an assistant? Do me a favor and give it some serious thought. Does that even make sense?"

I might as well have been standing there without my pants down, completely exposed. How did she manage to make me feel like an ass when I was the one who was supposed to be putting her on the spot? "What are you saying?" I asked, serious now.

She released a shaky breath through her nose, like a bull ready to charge. "I guess good old Clyde forgot to mention the part where he had the conversation with me in his hotel room at the Beverly Hilton. He had asked me up for lunch. It didn't take long for me to figure out *I* was on the menu. He wanted to talk about 'my career.' " She made air quotes with her fingers.

The unimaginative bastard. "What did you do?"

"I quit, obviously," she snapped. "Not before I had to kick him in the nuts to get him off me."

My father knew Clyde. They had been friends for years. How many times had I noticed him patting a girl's ass as she walked past? And there was that Christmas party at Mom and Dad's when I was a kid, where I watched from the staircase as he emerged from the powder room, followed by a girl who only stared at the floor as she bolted from my parents' house without saying a word to anyone.

"What?" she challenged. "You don't want to believe it? I bet the good guy would never do anything like that, right?"

"Don't put words in my mouth," I warned, and something about my tone snapped her mouth shut and wiped the sarcastic sneer from her face. "I believe you. And I'm sorry that happened. Really. You never have to worry about that here, though if anybody pulls any shit with you, I want you to let me know immediately. Do you understand?"

Her eyelids fluttered, and her cheeks went pink, but she nodded slowly.

"I guess that's where your reputation came from, then?" I asked, regretting that I threw it in her face.

"Not completely. You mentioned wanting to work

with Eric Danvers." For the first time, her gaze darted away from me. It had the strangest effect. It was like being released from some sort of spell that had held me in place. "I've worked with Eric Danvers. I also dated Eric Danvers," she added. "We were supposed to get engaged once *Road to Glory* was finished. To be honest with you, I knew before final edits that we were never going to have a future together. Professionally or otherwise. Don't ask me to get into it," she warned, holding up a hand which she then ran over her hair, still in its bun with loose auburn strands now framing her face from all her exertion.

"I hate him and would dance on his grave if he died tomorrow, but certain things are personal," she continued. "All I can say is he stole that film from me. He stole the credit. He stole that fucking award at Cannes too. That was mine," she insisted, her teeth gritted, her eyes glittering with something close to madness. Or was it simply betrayal?

What happened to ambition when it got turned on its head?

"You're serious?" I asked. Her head bobbed, and I didn't know if she was going to smash something on the floor or burst into tears. It could have gone either way based on the emotions washing over her face.

"I honestly don't know why I told you that," she confessed in a shaking voice. "I'm embarrassed. I trusted him. It wasn't enough for him to take credit for my work. He had to sabotage any sort of future I might have in this town. He had to get out in front of me, make up a story about how we clashed or something when he was the loser who couldn't handle his shit," she concluded, swiveling the chair away until she was staring out the window to her back.

"I'm glad you told me." Her honesty left me wanting to leave everything out on the table too—the trouble the studio was in, how it was dependent upon this project, having something positive to show the Board when it came time for the annual meeting.

That was different. It wasn't entirely my story to tell. What if word got out? I didn't know if this woman was trustworthy enough to keep a secret like that. All she had to do was whisper to one of her friends, and facing a scandal was too risky. It would tank us long before the end of the fiscal year.

"So, now we've cleared the air," she concluded. "What happens next?"

"What happens next is we make the best fucking picture we can. Full steam ahead. Let's get this thing done." Something had shifted. We were on the same team now.

It was more than that. Whatever wall was between us crumbled just enough for me to see the person beneath her prickly, antagonistic shell. I didn't realize it until she turned in the chair to reveal a wide, radiant smile and eyes that now shone with excitement. There was a real, wounded person in there. And if she had been the brains behind *Road to Glory*, she had a hell of a future in front of her.

A future I wanted to be part of, if only professionally. If we made a movie with the same sort of buzz *Road* had built without millions behind its publicity, there was no stopping me from ushering the studio into a new era, an era I could stamp my name on the way Dad had stamped his name on the studio after taking over from his father.

"All right," she agreed. I watched her jaw tighten in determination. "But I'm going to need an apartment. I'm tired of living out of my suitcase."

"Done. Your job tomorrow is to spend the morning looking for a place. All I need is a copy of the signed lease."

A pair of delicate eyebrows shot up. "You're serious?"

So that was all it took to impress her?

"As a heart attack. So start looking. I'll expect an answer by noon tomorrow. After that, your job is to scout locations. I want a full list by the time we get together for dinner tomorrow night at my house. I'll send you the details in the morning."

"Wait!" she called after me once I was in the hall, but it was too late. I was already moving, more determined than ever to get this done. The fire in my chest was now in my gut, pushing me onward.

"Can't hear you," I called out from my office, chuckling at her loud groan while wondering why the hell it smelled like sage in there.

4

———

SUMMER

"This is all wrong." I grabbed the hem of my sundress and pulled it over my head, balling it up and throwing it on the floor of what was going to be my motel room for one more night. First thing tomorrow, Claudia and I would load everything up into the back of her old Chevy to move into the apartment on Wilshire we'd found this morning.

It had been a whirlwind. Last night was spent searching through listings after the impromptu meeting with Lex. We were almost giddy with the possibilities while sharing a bottle of chardonnay. "Might as well shoot your shot," Claudia had pointed out more than once as we scrolled through eye-popping listings. Some of those apartments cost in one month what I had spent on my first car.

But she had a point. What was the worst thing Lex could say? *No, it's too expensive?* The idea made me giggle. We hadn't known each other for long, but I could read a person. It meant swallowing his pride and admitting he couldn't afford it, which he'd never do. Not a man like him, with something to prove, not to mention his deep pockets.

Still, after we had toured the two-bedroom, two-bathroom apartment in the heart of Beverly Hills, I had called Lex's direct number with my heart in my throat. Yet when I quoted the price, he didn't balk for a second. "That sounds reasonable. Have the property manager forward me the agreement, and I'll have my assistant handle the details."

And that was it. It was that simple. It wasn't even ten o'clock yet, which meant we had plenty of time to scout shooting locations. I already had a handful in mind, confirming how perfect they were while Claudia and I drove from place to place.

There was only one problem as I dug through the few decent outfits I owned, hoping to look presentable tonight. It was the fact that Lex Landry wanted me to meet him at his house in the Hills for dinner.

"Would you relax? It doesn't mean anything," Claudia reminded me for maybe the hundredth time since he had dropped that bombshell.

I called to tell him I had a list of locations, and he had announced he'd send a driver to pick me up at eight o'clock and drive me to his house, where we'd go over the locations and the shooting schedule.

"Why can't we do this in public?" I asked, pulling out a pair of linen pants that needed a quick ironing. "I told him what happened with Clyde. I'm not supposed to think there's something fishy about this?"

"He figures you'll trust him because he knows what happened," she countered. "You said he seemed pretty pissed off about it."

"He did," I admitted.

"And honestly," she continued, picking up my sundress off the floor and shaking it out. "What are you supposed to do? Meet up at some fancy restaurant and spread a bunch of work across the table? It's a working dinner. You either do it here, at the studio, or his house."

"Why do you always have to make so much damn sense?" I muttered, holding the pants up in front of me and checking out my reflection in the mirror. "I don't know. Does this look right?"

"I think your instincts were right with the dress."

"I don't want him thinking I dressed up for him."

"Maybe you shouldn't have blown out your hair and put on makeup," she pointed out in a gentle voice, chuckling.

"I'm wearing mascara and lip gloss. That's not makeup."

"Sure, whatever you say. Wear the dress," she concluded, flopping onto the bed and picking up the remote to turn on the television. "And consider yourself lucky. I'm looking forward to Chinese delivery tonight."

"Don't even pretend Chinese isn't your favorite."

"When I'm not eating it in some crappy motel," she muttered. "I'm sure it would taste a little better if I were at a house in the Hills with a wealthy movie producer."

"Don't make it sound like something it's not." Because I knew she wouldn't let it go, I put the powder blue dress back on, telling myself to ignore the way the tiny pleats under the bust line pushed my boobs up and out. I couldn't help myself as I adjusted them, fretting a little.

"Why are you so afraid of being beautiful?" she asked.

"Because it can be a liability," I fired back without thinking. Our eyes met in the mirror, and I shrugged. "We've both met men like him. They see a pair of boobs, and their brains click off. I wanna be taken seriously."

"That doesn't mean you have to cover yourself up all the time. You look really nice," she told me with a thumbs up. "And the car will be here any minute, so put your shoes on."

"Wow, what would I do without you?" I asked, rolling my eyes. "I might've walked out barefoot. Thanks, *Mommy*." She only laughed, flipping through channels while I silently panicked.

I'd told her about the talk we had last night back at the studio office. What I didn't tell her was the way I felt when he left. He had surprised me. Maybe I had underestimated him, figuring he'd laugh off my story about Clyde. The man had been in the industry for fifty years, and he was the sort of guy people didn't accuse of things if they wanted to get a job in this town.

But Lex had accepted it without question. He had been angry, for my sake. He had looked disgusted when I told him about Eric. And he was determined to make a good movie. He had skin in the game, the same as I did, and it wasn't only financial. He was worried about more than the bottom line.

It was refreshing.

At exactly eight o'clock, there was a knock on the door. I opened it with my heart in my throat and was greeted by a man in a dark suit. "Miss Strawbridge? Mr. Landry sent me to pick you up."

"Have fun and chill out!" Claudia whispered as I grabbed the shoulder bag that held my binder, laptop, and everything I'd put together so far for the movie.

My knees shook as I followed the driver to the long, sleek limo. He'd sent a goddamn limousine. Who was he trying to impress?

All right, so maybe I was a little impressed as I ducked inside and sank into a leather seat. Maybe it wasn't completely evil to make a lot of money from movies. Not that I would admit that to Lex. He still had a long way to go before I was convinced he was a thoroughly decent guy.

One thing I knew for sure as the car finished rolling up a winding road was the man had a more than decent house. Plate glass windows meant a view of the sprawling interior, while discreet lighting shows off meticulous landscaping. I'd bet my entire paycheck for the movie that there was a big pool around back and a breath-taking view.

I'd lived in a trailer until I was ten, sharing a tiny room with two sisters. It was only when Dad had landed a teaching job at UCLA that we were able to move into a house with more than two bedrooms, not that it was much more comfortable. I was raised to hate everything about this lifestyle.

Climbing out of a limousine, walking up the flag-stone path of a Hollywood Hills mansion to have dinner with a studio executive. It meant selling out, sacrificing my art on the altar of money.

Was it wrong to want to make this work on my terms? Did I have to go through life scraping by if it meant being an artist?

The front door swung open, and I was treated to the sight of a freshly showered Lex. His dark brown hair turned black with the water that still dripped and soaked into his pale green T-shirt. A pair of gray sweatpants completed the outfit. He was on the phone, scowling, barely waving me in before turning and padding barefoot across the hardwood floor.

And there I was, wearing a sundress so thin that my nipples went hard in the air condition-ing. I tried to ignore them and the sense of being overdressed while following Lex past a sunken living room and a room that had to be his office, with a desk, computer, and a window behind it that looked out over the big pool I had imagined.

"Give me a second." He pulled the phone away from his ear, scowling as he muted it. "I've been running late all day after a meeting went an hour too long. My cook left salad and antipasto in the refrigerator. Kitchen's that way, help yourself." He jerked his chin toward the kitchen up ahead while heading into his office.

What the hell was this? A power play? Forget a sundress or even linen slacks. I should've thrown on my workout clothes if this were the respect I'd get tonight. Instead of setting the food out like a member of his staff, I pulled out my laptop and binder and began spreading out on the white marble island.

The room was sort of clinical in all white, but it probably glowed in the morning when sunshine streamed in through the huge windows lining the back wall.

I was reviewing a task list when I heard Lex's soft footsteps. "I only threw this on after my shower so I could make that call," he explained behind me. "Give me a minute to make myself presentable."

"No need," I replied without turning away from

my work. Even the addition of the folder he placed near me didn't break my focus. "You look fine. I didn't get the food out, though. That's not in my contract."

He growled and muttered something about splitting hairs as he went to the refrigerator and pulled out items. I saw him out of the corner of my eye and wished his ass didn't look quite so delectable when he bent to look for something on one of the lower shelves.

But it was the way his dick moved under those sweatpants when he turned to the side that set my cheeks on fire. Was he wearing underwear? Well, I had told him not to bother getting changed, hadn't I? My pulse picked up speed, but I fought to ignore it as Lex set various things on the marble countertop. "Wine?" he asked, bending to open a door on his side of the island.

I needed to keep a clear head, but I needed to ease my nerves more. "Sure. Thanks." Looking up from my binder, I found an array of meats, cheeses, olives, and spreads on one platter. On another, there was grilled chicken and vegetables. He added a long baguette to the spread, then opened a bottle of white wine.

"Let's talk actresses," I suggested, bypassing the

meats in favor of tearing off a hunk of bread and pairing it with a piece of sharp cheddar. The flavor exploded across my tongue. *Note to self. Buy some good cheese.* Now that I had a full-size refrigerator in my new apartment, I could fill it with my favorites. Another perk of being gainfully employed.

"Let me pour the wine first," he countered, shaking his head a little as he pulled out a pair of glasses. "Take a breath."

"You take a breath. I'll cast this movie."

He turned slowly away from the cabinet above the deep sink. "Oh. That. I wanted to talk with you about that tonight."

"Here I am. Let's talk." I popped a briny olive into my mouth and quickly went for another. It had been a busy day, and I hadn't taken much time to eat.

He set a glass down in front of me, meeting my gaze. There'd have to come a point where I would get over the fluttering in my stomach whenever that happened. I could only pretend to ignore it for so long, and the cold wine didn't do much to cool the heat in my chest, either.

"We've already been in talks with a cast for the film. Rather, we arranged it prior to our first meeting." He waved a hand between us, sipping from his glass.

I had to be hearing things. Was I dreaming? "You're already casting?" I asked, waiting for him to laugh and say it was all a joke. Except he didn't. It wasn't.

"The folder I brought in contains the headshots of our cast, along with everything we need to know about them... their requests, any precautions we need to take, like with Danica Cole and her bee allergy. We need the medic on hand during her outdoor shoots, just in case."

Danica Cole. A big-breasted blonde without much obvious talent who the industry had been cramming down the world's collective throat for the past year. I couldn't remember a single name of one of her projects, she was that forgettable.

I opened the folder with a trembling hand, my entire body filling with dread and a sense of defeat. This was all a joke from the beginning. I was never in control, was I?

"We need a sure thing here, Summer." He put together a small plate for himself, talking as he did. "We need big names, box office track records."

I chewed a slice of grilled squash but didn't taste a thing as I flipped through the images of familiar actors. "You cast my movie without me. We have a cast, and I'm only finding out about it now?"

"Don't take it personally."

That was the cherry on top of my shit sundae. The way he said that and sounded like he meant it. Rather than open my mouth and let every ounce of my rage come pouring out, I slowly drank my wine until the glass was empty, searching for something to say that wouldn't get me fired or result in me breaking down in tears. "I knew it." I finally sighed, even laughing softly. "In the end, it doesn't matter if we make the best movie possible. Those were pretty words you fed me. Only one thing makes a difference to people like you."

The fucker had the nerve to roll his eyes and was lucky I didn't throw something at him for it. "Please, can we be adults about this? You're about a heartbeat away from taking it too far."

The sanctimonious prick. I was almost blind with rage, and he wanted to talk about being adults? "Another cowardly move," I whispered, watching his tan complexion go darker. Did I hurt the baby's feelings? Poor thing. "Whatever it takes, so long as you help the Hollywood machine pump out the same old bullshit. Have you ever respected your audience for a minute, or do you figure they'll pay either way?"

He threw his hands into the air, barking out a

laugh that echoed throughout the room. "Give it up, already!"

"Not when we both know it's true!"

"Let's get something straight. Just because I didn't go to film school or spend years scraping and fighting in the trenches for my 'art'..." he made air quotes around the word art, which only made me grind my teeth, "... that doesn't mean I don't care about the process. I'm not looking to make some formulaic, brainless blockbuster, Summer."

"What are you looking to make? Because all of your so-called casting suggestions have been predictable and uninspired. What else am I supposed to think?" I shoved the folder across the counter when I would've liked to cram it down his throat.

Slamming a palm against the counter, he growled out, "You're supposed to think I want this movie to make money, goddammit."

"Of course!" I barked out a laugh. "Because that's all that matters. *Money.*"

"It sort of helps. It's helping you stay in a gorgeous apartment for the next six months, isn't it?"

"Don't hold that over my head," I warned.

He lifted a shoulder. "I was only calling you out on your hypocrisy."

"My hypocrisy?" I asked, laughing again. "Oh, get over yourself. If I'm going to be beholden to you all because you've signed a short-term lease for me, you can spare us both. I'd rather live in a motel for the next six months than have to kiss your ass just because of an apartment."

"You are more than welcome to." His stony face and steely-eyed stare sent apprehension skittering down my spine. He was serious. He wasn't going to back down.

Neither was I. It wasn't what I did. "Fine. I will. I wouldn't want to owe you anything if it meant sacrificing my vision."

"There you go with your vision," he muttered, waving a hand. "Has anyone ever taught you the meaning of the word compromise?"

"Oh, sure," I retorted. "I compromised by doing ninety percent of the work on *Road to Glory* and got zero percent of the credit. Yeah, that worked out really well."

"You're going to have to let go of that."

"Thanks for the advice."

He growled, drawing a deep breath through clenched teeth. His smoldering brown eyes went nearly black. There was something wild about him, but I wasn't afraid. Instinctively, I knew this wouldn't turn into something ugly or violent.

No, it wasn't fear that left goose bumps covering my arms. It was something else, something I barely recognized and sort of resented myself for. How could I not respond to the energy in the air and his heavy breathing? My breath quickened while my pulse picked up speed.

And when our eyes met, a bolt of energy raced through me like I had stuck my finger in an outlet. I was surprised my hair didn't stand on end.

"There is a middle ground," he gritted out, his teeth still clenched. "Between fulfilling your vision and making the sort of choices that will help this movie make money. That's why, even though you know a completely unknown and untested actress might be a good fit for a role, you might be better off going with a bigger name who has already proven herself more than capable. Just because she's not exactly what you had envisioned doesn't mean she's the wrong choice. Your vision isn't the only one that matters."

"You can't always have everything your way." Fuck Eric for popping up in my head when he did. That patronizing tone of his. Always knowing best, practically patting me on the head like a spoiled child. We

had gone to school together, for God's sake, and were exactly the same age. Yet he had the nerve to act like an expert.

I stepped down from the stool I was perched on, slowly rounding the island, glaring at him. He was hot, but he was an arrogant prick. I needed to focus on the second part more than the first. "I was hired to do a job. How do you expect me to do my best when you throw a cast at me without my input or approval?"

"When are you going to realize you're not in a position to give approval? You are untested, untried. Frankly, you're lucky to have this opportunity," he concluded with a wave of his hand, though he might as well have slapped me with it.

"Is this the part where you encourage me to suck your dick as thanks? I mean, here we are," I reminded him, spreading my arms to the sides. "Alone in your house. And all you can do is remind me of how grateful I should be for the scraps you're throwing around."

"Scraps?" He threw his head back and laughed, making my face go hot with frustration along with embarrassment.

All of it swirled together and hardened into something more familiar. Rage. "Yes!" I snapped.

"That's what I said. This is a great opportunity on the surface, but that's it. Otherwise, I'll have to smile, nod, shake hands, play nice and basically lie."

"Nobody's asking you to do any of that. In fact, Summer Strawbridge, I'm starting to think you're not worth the fucking trouble." He slapped his hands against the marble counter again and turned away from me, his broad shoulders heaving while he hung his head between them.

"Okay. Fine. You're doing me a favor," I muttered, grabbing things at random with my shaking hands and shoving them into my bag. To think, I cared how I looked tonight. I wanted to make a good impression. When would I learn it didn't matter how hard I tried?

He snorted in derision. "That's right. Run away. Shit got too hard, somebody told you no, and you're going to bounce."

"If that's what you need to tell yourself, go right ahead," I gritted out. "I'm sure the brain-dead idiots around town will believe it. Critical thinking has never been their specialty."

He raised his head. "All right. Wait." It was like taking a few seconds to think made him see the error of his ways. Good. But I wasn't that easy to convince.

When I kept packing my bag, he wedged himself

between me and the counter. "I said wait, dammit. Let's take a step back. We both said things—"

"I meant every word," I told him as he came up with some empty platitude. "This entire situation has been bait-and-switch. First, you fuck with my scheduling. Now, you tell me the movie's already been cast. This is a figurehead position. That's not what I signed on for."

"Why is everything black and white all the time?" Folding his arms meant his biceps bulged right in my line of sight. I had to force myself not to gape at them.

"Why can't you admit I'm getting the shaft in all of this? It's not fair." I stared up at him, unblinking, daring him to look away. If he had any decency, I would see shame in those coffee-colored orbs. There was nothing there but arrogance like I had expected.

"At the risk of sounding geriatric, kid, life isn't fair. This industry is anything but fair."

"You know... I know all about that," I whispered.

"For fuck's sake, take an opportunity when it presents itself. Don't shoot yourself in the foot." His eyes searched my face, his mouth working silently before he found the right words. "If you really did direct and edit *Road to Glory*, you're too damn good to sabotage yourself. Don't waste this opportunity."

"What if it doesn't feel like an opportunity?" Something was wrong. I felt a little dizzy and giddy, but it had nothing to do with the wine and everything to do with beautiful eyes and sensual mouth. Something about it left me staring while an honest-to-God party erupted in my panties. My knees went weak, and for one breathless, insane moment, I pictured myself leaning against him for support. Maybe even touching my nose to his chest to breathe in his spicy cologne— masculine, like leather, spice, and tobacco.

This was a mistake. I should never have come, and I definitely shouldn't have accepted the wine. It would be too easy to forget every principle I ever had in this man's presence—his hot, commanding, overwhelming presence.

His throat worked while his gaze drifted between my eyes and mouth. "Then it looks like I'm going to have to drag you through this kicking and screaming," he murmured, and suddenly, he was a lot closer, leaning down, filling my world with his chiseled face. "It's your choice, Strawbridge."

How was I supposed to resist this? How, when every cell of my body cried out for him to finally end this breathless, heart-pounding tension? He looked at my mouth one last time, and I bit my lip, waiting, hanging on his every breath.

He blinked hard, shaking his head a little. "Hang on," he muttered, his voice thick, like a man waking from a dream when he didn't know he was asleep in the first place.

Hang on, indeed. "Right," I whispered, trembling, my heart bursting out of my chest. What the hell were we doing? Was I seriously considering testing the taste of his lips? Damn wine. That had to be the problem.

He backed up, hands clenched at his sides. "That got a little too heated," he grunted out, strained.

"It's not a big deal," I muttered, slinging the bag over my shoulder and looking at the floor. I still couldn't look at him. "But I really have to go, anyway."

"What about—"

"We'll work it all out." I practically ran from the kitchen like it was on fire, my head down, my face burning with humiliation. "Can your driver take me home, please?"

"Of course. Summer, please," he insisted as he followed me. "Can we at least try to reach an understanding?"

"It's a waste of time," I replied, stopping at the

front door and turning to find him looking apologetic, maybe even remorseful. "We're not going to see eye-to-eye. You know how much this movie means to me. I know how much it means to you. Let's keep that in mind, all right?"

"All right." He held up his hands, surrendering. "You have the cast list. Rehearsals start next week."

Dammit. He had me trapped now. I was too desperate to get the hell out of there and avoid further humiliation to hang around and argue about a rushed rehearsal schedule. I had to accept it since nothing mattered more at the moment than getting far away from him.

What a shame his driver couldn't take me to the other side of the planet since nothing short of that would ease my disappointment as I hurried out of the house, almost blinded by tears.

I'd never get what I wanted, how I wanted it.

At the moment, it seemed Lex Landry was part of that.

5

—————

LEX

By Friday morning, the end of our first week, it was time to check in with the old men who kept the studio's wheels greased with the money they threw our way.

"Everything is going according to plan." If I didn't stop forcing a smile, my face would freeze this way. It was starting to look more like a pained grimace. "We're due to start rehearsals Monday. It will be a little rushed," I admitted as lightly as possible. "But I have nothing but faith in the talent we've managed to round up."

One of the studio's longtime investors offered an indulgent laugh. "Your father sure has a keen eye for picking the right people for a role."

My teeth ground as my smile hardened. I was

looking at a screen full of old faces, sagging jowls, permanent scowls, and more than a little confusion when it came to the finer points of navigating a Zoom call. We were running ten minutes behind, thanks to so-called technical difficulties. Really, the five men on the call didn't have the first clue how to do much of anything without their wives or assistants handling it for them.

"Yes, Dad pitched in," I gritted out, silently seething. "I know by now it's a bad idea to ignore his instinct."

Those smug bastards. Sitting back in their offices or on their back patios beneath umbrellas, all they had to do was wait around and collect on their investment. They'd complain like hell if they lost money and act like kings of the world if the film was a success, as if they had anything to do with it beyond writing a check.

"It does look like a very ambitious timeline." Pierce Williams, the oldest and most sour of the group, narrowed his faded eyes and leaned in until his face filled his screen. "Are you sure all of this can be done in such a short amount of time?"

It was a normal question. *Hold it together.* "I have nothing but confidence in our team," I assured him.

"Even that little hellcat you've got directing for

you?" Pierce chuckled, setting off a chain reaction until all of the men staring at me through their respective machines did the same. Now I understood something I never had before. There was a difference between people laughing because something was funny and the nasty, knowing laughter that now grated my nerves.

"Miss Strawbridge has been nothing but a solid, responsible, and energetic partner in all of this." A partner I hadn't spoken to for several days, not since the disastrous dinner at my house on Tuesday night. We had exchanged a few texts and emails, none of which contained anything personal. She reported back to me after meeting the actors. I confirmed filming permits, which had been fast-tracked and approved.

At least I knew I hadn't scared her away from the project—an idea that had kept me up half the night after she left. What if she decided to quit?

"So long as you don't let her walk all over you," Pierce advised. "You know how it is nowadays. You look at a woman the wrong way for more than half a second, and all of a sudden, she's screaming assault."

I was going to need a shower after this call was finished. My skin was crawling, and the memory of Summer's story about what happened with Clyde didn't help things. I believed her. I had from the start. But would they if they were in my place?

Why did it matter? They were the money, nothing more. I needed to get out of my head. There were still plenty of calls and follow-ups to handle today, all in preparation for our short rehearsal period next week.

Thanking the men for their time, I gratefully ended the call and leaned back in my chair, blowing out a heavy sigh. I was a sponge that had been wrung out, completely dry, but it was over for now. I had convinced our backers that everything was moving along according to schedule. So long as I kept them happy and quiet, we'd be all right. I needed to believe that. Otherwise, I couldn't shake the sense of being at the broken controls of a runaway train.

After taking a few laps in the pool, I showered off and fixed myself a little lunch based on what the cook left in the refrigerator before taking her day off today. There was pasta salad and a platter of grilled chicken, so I combined some of both before strolling into the living room and turning on the television.

It had been a long time since I kicked back like this, with my bare feet on the coffee table, looking for something mindless to distract me from what had been bouncing around in my head for days. I paused on a news show, setting the remote aside to eat a few mouthfuls of the delicious salad Lisette had put together for me. She knew I liked to have things lying around that I might grab easily, and this was one of my favorite dishes.

What a shame the taste soured in my mouth when the entertainment news queued up, and the bleached blonde on the screen chirped, "There's a new name at Sunrise Pictures. Eric Danvers, director of Cannes darling *Road to Glory*, has inked a three-picture deal with the prominent studio."

A photo replaced her smiling face, and now the idea of taking another bite was unthinkable. I sat up, leaving the bowl on the coffee table, staring at Clyde Harris and Eric Danvers as they stood together in front of the Sunrise Pictures sign spanning the gates in front of their studio.

I had seen photos of Danvers, mostly while I researched potential directors for this project. It was incredible how perception could change. Now, knowing what I knew, his smile was slimy, his eyes cold. He had the face of somebody I'd like to punch. Some people were like that. They had punchable faces.

She's going to be upset about this. It was a

surprising thought, coming out of nowhere while I imagined the satisfaction of my fist connecting with his square chin. Some people just begged for it.

Instead of looking for something else to put on, I switched off the television and stared at the ceiling. I had planned to recuperate a little today once the Zoom call ended. We were about to hit the ground running with no brakes, and it felt necessary to unwind before doing that to get my head in a good place.

It seemed like the world had other plans for me. I pulled up Summer's contact in my phone on my way back to the kitchen, where I left my bowl in the refrigerator to eat later. I didn't want to waste it, even if I couldn't stomach the thought of swallowing another bite when imagining the damage I could do to Eric Danvers' face.

I wasn't expecting the unfamiliar female voice that chirped, "You've reached Summer Strawbridge's phone."

It threw me off for a second, but I replied, "Who is this? I need to speak to Summer."

"This is her assistant, Claudia. Is this Mr. Landry? It's nice to meet you."

"Same here, Claudia." She sounded cute, but she was wasting my time. "Can I speak to Summer?"

There was a little not-so-quiet murmuring going on in the background. It was the sort of murmuring that told me the person doing it was unhappy. Now I understood why I got handed off to the assistant. When she saw my name on the phone, Summer probably told Claudia to take it.

"Tell her I thought she had more guts," I added, raising my voice in the hope she would hear me. "I didn't think she'd hide behind an assistant."

Not three seconds passed. "What the hell kind of bullshit is that supposed to mean?" Summer spat into the phone. I didn't even mind her cussing me out when she was so easy to provoke.

"Oh, so you are available," I replied. "I wanted to know—"

"I am doing the work of three or four different people right now," she informed me. "And we're starting rehearsals in three days. And you're calling to pick a fight?"

"No, that's not why I called. I was hoping for a status report."

"If you want a status report, you're going to have to come to the studio to get one. I'm wading through a mountain of work. Maybe you can help me," she added with a derisive snort.

I shouldn't give her what she wants. I don't jump

every time she snaps her fingers. That was true, but it was also true that the girl could be a real bitch who knew how to push buttons I wasn't aware existed. Challenging me to come down and meet with her, very clearly accusing me of being unable to handle the work *and* in front of her assistant, no less.

So much for my relaxing day.

"I'll be there in fifteen," I announced. "Prepare yourself to carve a few minutes out of your busy schedule for me."

SHE WASN'T KIDDING about the mountain of work. There were storyboards propped up against the walls. A huge corkboard covered with photos, head-shots, renderings of set pieces in the middle of being built for some of our later shots. For the time being, we would focus on exterior shots, which comprised a solid percentage of the script.

And in the middle of the storm stood Summer. It didn't seem to matter that she played soft, soothing music or was burning incense that made my nose wrinkle in distaste. None of it seemed to soothe her almost frantic energy as she hustled back and forth, switching storyboards before standing back with her hands clasped on top of her head. Her long, auburn locks were free of their usual bun and hung halfway to her waist, flowing like a shimmering waterfall down her back.

What I would do to imagine those smooth, silky strands wrapped around my fist as I fuck her from behind. *Fuck, Lex, get your shit together.*

"Please, tell me you found the tea." She turned, hope etched across her face, but that hope dried up when she saw me standing in the doorway instead of her assistant. "Oh..." She sighed.

It was not the best or warmest greeting I'd ever received, but par for the course. "You weren't expecting me?" I asked, plastering on a smile I did not feel. How could she be so damn brittle and prickly and still turn me on the way she did?

"I thought you were Claudia," she replied, turning back to her work. "I sent her out to find a specific tea I like to drink when I'm feeling stressed. I told her to grab every single package she might find."

"I didn't know you had an assistant working with you."

Her shoulders lifted. "Is there something wrong with that?"

"Not at all. I'm glad you have somebody to help

out." I was starting to forget why I had called her in the first place. I could've kicked myself for being a stupid ass. She didn't need to be coddled. Hell, if I tried, she'd sooner bite my head off.

"You are obviously very busy." I approached slowly, studying the storyboards outlining key scenes, presenting the way Summer had envisioned the script. They weren't highly detailed, but they were good. "Who drew these?"

"I did, for the most part."

"No shit?" She shook her head. "Where did you find the time?"

"Find the time?" She barked out a laugh. "It's sleep I'm struggling to find time for right now." Her hair shimmered when she ran her fingers through it, begging to be touched. ~~The way I touched it in my kitchen, sinking my hands deep.~~

Desire was a fucked-up thing. It seemed I couldn't stop swinging from one extreme to the other between wanting to kill her and needing to fuck the sass out of her.

"Careful," I warned, fists clenched in my pockets to keep from reaching out. The sight of the circles under her eyes helped calm some of the fire. She wasn't exaggerating, and this was a dangerous road to travel. "We still have a long way to go. I can't have you working yourself into exhaustion and ending up in the hospital."

"I can handle stress. I told you. I had to step in and handle *Road to Glory* on my own." She folded her arms, sighing softly, staring at the corkboard. "I guess you heard the news. I know word travels fast."

"About that asshole and his three-picture deal? I heard about it earlier."

Her shoulders rose and fell. "Please tell me you weren't calling to check up on me," she murmured, her voice flat.

"Based on your history with him, I thought it made sense to check in with you."

Snickering, she turned her head, eyes rolling. "Because you wouldn't want your precious movie to go off schedule, right?"

Why did I bother giving a shit? "Yes, because that's all I care about," I muttered, looking her up and down. "You don't know anything about me, Summer."

She was already itching for an argument—that much was obvious—and I had given her all the ammo she needed. Eyes flashing, she snapped, "I know that at the end of the day, dollar signs are what matter most. Don't patronize me and pretend there's more to it than that. This is a business, and we both know it."

I couldn't win with her. Why was I trying? "If you're fine, I'll take your word on it. So long as everything is ready for Monday." The sooner I got away from her, the better. Eventually, one of us would destroy this project by saying something we couldn't take back.

"It will be ready," she assured me as I backed away. "Even if I don't sleep a wink between now and then."

"You realize there's no gold medal for self-sacrifice in this industry, right?"

"Trust me. I have no illusions." She shook her head as she walked to her desk to search for something in the pile of folders and binders there. "I know self-sacrifice doesn't get rewarded. Only being willing to kiss ass and suck a little dick when necessary."

I stiffened at her tone and the underlying accusations. "You know you don't have to worry about that here." There was no reason to defend myself, yet something compelled me to. Make sure she didn't get the wrong idea. Why else would she mention sucking dick if she wasn't thinking about it?

"I don't have time for this." Something about the

harshness in her words and the hard set of her jaw touched a deep part of me that intrigued, challenged, and infuriated me. There she was again, acting like her word was law and to hell with anybody who thought otherwise. She took one measured step after another, staring me down. "This movie means a lot to you? Guess what? I don't have the safety net you have. If this is ruined, I'm ruined. You can always move on with all of your money and your connections, and you'll be fine. I don't have any of those things. Do you understand?" By the time she finished, we were almost toe-to-toe. Her chest heaved, drawing my attention, but I was more captivated by the fire in her eyes. It was the sort of fire I wanted to put out but imagined allowing it to burn.

"You keep reminding me," I replied. "Is there anything new you can offer? Anything else riding on this? Or are you going to keep beating your dead horse until it's nothing but red mist?"

Her mouth fell open a second before a bright voice rang out behind me. "I bought four boxes of tea and packs of those seaweed sheets you like to snack on."

Claudia. "Saved by the assistant," I muttered, catching a glimpse of Summer's scowl as she turned to meet the newcomer.

She was even cuter than her voice let on, with a curvy body and a halo of black curls. Extending a hand, I offered my most charming smile. I had to, or else she might see how close I was to losing my grip. "Hi. I'm Lex Landry. And you must be the most patient woman alive."

6

———

SUMMER

"This is it. Are you ready?"

Was I ready? I knew Claudia's question was rhetorical. There was no choice but to be ready. This was day one, our first day of shooting after a week of rushed rehearsals. All in all, though I would've liked a little more time to get to know my cast and for them to get to know each other, I was feeling positive and energized in the minutes before our first shot. The hours I'd spent meditating on it were helping.

But not quite enough since I was also a bundle of nerves and pretty sure I was going to pee myself since my bladder decided to act all nervous. I knew what I was doing. I had done it before. Okay, so I was working at a much higher level than I ever had, and this was a much bigger deal than an indie film none of us was very sure would go anywhere. That was more of a passion project.

This? This had consequences.

"Oh, you're kidding me." Claudia's soft muttering yanked me back into the present moment, where she was staring over my shoulder with narrowed eyes.

I followed the direction she was staring in, and my stomach dropped. "What is he doing here?" I asked in a strained whisper as Lex Landry climbed out of a ridiculously splashy sports car parked outside the border created by trucks, vans, and the handful of tents set up to protect the cast from the sun between takes.

He looked infuriatingly good. That was the worst part. I might handle him looking over my shoulder so long as he didn't have to go and distract me by how goddamn handsome he was. The pale yellow of his polo shirt accentuated his deep tan, while the sleeves were barely big enough to contain his impressive biceps. He slid on a pair of aviators, sauntering our way, one hand in his pocket, strolling like a man without a care in the world. Like I didn't have enough on my mind, I'd have to wrestle whatever was causing the fluttering in my stomach whenever I looked at him.

"Oh, there he is." Danica Cole, my lead actress, nudged the girl standing closest to her and nodded in his direction. She leaned against the car she was supposed to be working on in this scene, folding her arms while clocking his every move. "God, I'd fuck him senseless if I had the chance. What do you think we have to do to get invited to a party at his house?"

Of course, if I were in her position, I might think the same thing. But then, I wasn't some desperate, grasping actress looking for a leg up.

"Down, girl." Claudia patted me on the shoulder when I managed to pry my attention away from Danica and found my best friend scowling. "You're not doing yourself any favors by looking like you're going to claw your lead actress' eyes out."

I opened my mouth, prepared to tell her I didn't look that way, but I probably did. Yes, I was a little irritated, but it was none of my business. Lex could sleep with whoever he wanted. No doubt he'd bed a girl like Danica, who looked like a supermodel even while wearing oil-smeared coveralls. He'd stay away from her if he were smart, but men were men. They only ignored their stupid dicks for so long.

"Coming around to make sure we're earning our money, Mr. Landry?" one of the crew members shouted, laughing.

"You know I have to stay on your ass, Keith," Lex shouted back. So they knew each other. Keith wasn't the only one, either. A handful of people wandered Lex's way, shaking his hand, and nobody was more surprised than me when he asked them personal questions about themselves or their families. He wasn't kidding when he said he grew up at the studio.

"He has a way with people," Claudia observed in a soft, approving voice. "I mean, would you expect a rich studio executive to know about a gaffer's kids?"

"Whatever, so he's a halfway decent guy." That was unfair. I knew he was better than that, at least from what he had shown me of himself. I hadn't told her about the talk we had, but this wasn't the time or place to go into personal feelings. I still didn't know why I never told her. We told each other everything, to the point where we overshared. A quarter-century of friendship meant there weren't many things that were off the table.

But for some reason, talking with Lex was private and personal. There was something about it I wanted to guard carefully. For the first time in this town, somebody had listened and understood, and it happened to be the last person I expected it from.

I raised the megaphone to my mouth. "Okay,

everybody. I need places." The boss was here. It was time to make sure he knew what his studio was paying for and for him to see I knew what I was doing.

I've got this. It's all in my head. Shot for shot, frame for frame, this is going to work. I took my place behind the monitor while the cast took their marks. A palpable energy filled the air, turning it electric as I pulled in a deep, steadying breath before calling out, "Action!"

Funny. Most people would probably lose their shit after shouting that word. It meant this was it, it was real, it was happening. No turning back. All it did was calm me. A sense of peace washed over me all at once. I was where I belonged. I knew what I was doing, and it was what I was born to do.

I almost forgot Lex was standing no more than ten feet away, watching me instead of the work going on in front of the camera. How did I know?

I felt him.

By the time the clock struck four and the crew was in the process of clearing the area after shooting, I was exhausted in the best way possible. It had been an interesting day full of working out little hiccups that couldn't be predicted. The sort that only came up in the moment. Minor dialogue changes, blocking issues, not to mention a strong gust of wind that had blown dirt and sand in everybody's faces and resulted in time spent fixing hair and makeup.

But the first day was in the can, and I couldn't pretend I wasn't flying high. I'd never have another first day of shooting my first major Hollywood movie. What a shame there wasn't a way to bottle this feeling.

I had even managed to forget Lex's presence as my awareness narrowed down to a single focal point. I was in the zone, completely locked in. Only now, after hours of shooting, did I remember he was watching from the background all along. His cherry red Maserati was still parked where he'd left it. Who would've thought he'd stay all day?

"Great work!" he called out to the gaffer and key grip as they finished taking down the lighting equipment. He then turned to take in the rest of the cast and crew, cupping his hands around his mouth so his voice would carry. "Thank you all so much for giving it your everything today."

My heart lurched when he approached. What was he going to do? Hopefully, he wasn't looking for a hug or anything personal. Instead, he made a *come hither* motion with his hand. "Can I use that?" he asked, grabbing for the bullhorn sitting on an empty chair beside me.

The way he inserted himself into the situation shouldn't have made me grind my teeth, but they sure as hell were grinding when he turned the bullhorn on and addressed everyone. "I've reserved a room for us at Mystique tonight in West Hollywood. It's an opening party, and the entire cast and crew are welcome."

The excitement that rolled over the group had an interesting effect on me. I gritted my teeth harder, forcing a smile for the sake of everyone else. This was supposed to be my big, triumphant day, and he found a way to one-up me.

There was one person who knew me well enough to take one look at my face and sum up everything going on in my head. "Hey. Get over yourself," Claudia murmured, standing close to me.

"Mind your own business," I whispered, gathering my things while the crew chattered and asked for details. Eight o'clock, casual dress code, open bar was all they needed to hear.

"I'm sure this is supposed to be a kind, generous gesture," she whispered. Because why would she ever cut me some slack for once? That was the draw-back to working with somebody who knew me so well. She knew the right buttons to push and wasn't going to back down no matter how much crap I gave her.

"Yeah, a kind, generous gesture I'm going to have to show up for," I grumbled.

"I think it's a good idea." Suddenly, she stood up a little straighter, staring down at her phone, and I knew why almost before I heard his voice behind me.

"I hope you'll be joining us." When I lifted my head, ready to reply, I realized Lex wasn't talking to me. He was smiling at Claudia, whose cheeks went pink.

When she glanced my way, she gulped. "I think I can clear room in my schedule as long as my boss says it's okay."

Oh, so we were now joking and friendly, were we? Seeing them sharing a smile gave me the sort of feeling I used to get as a kid when my sisters' latest projects were praised while mine was overlooked. I felt like I wouldn't measure up and had to work twice as hard to prove myself. I couldn't imagine why that feeling overcame me at this particular moment.

I only knew it made my skin feel too tight and my insides too hot.

"That's fine with me," I announced, though neither of them had bothered bringing me into the conversation. "But I hope nobody minds if I can't make it. I have a lot of work to do to get ready for tomorrow."

"Oh, come on," Lex insisted as he lifted his sunglasses. His casual drawl made me wonder why he thought we were friendly enough for him to behave like this, like we were all one big, happy family. It had to be a matter of his image, making sure everybody saw him as the benevolent good guy. "Making an appearance for an hour isn't going to ruin your schedule."

"Says who?" I challenged with a tight smile that caused his dark eyes to narrow.

"Would you stop arguing?" Claudia whispered, but I pretended not to hear her.

"One hour." He held up a finger while an almost playful grin played over his lips. I really wished they didn't draw my attention like they did, and I wished even harder that I hadn't wondered what they tasted like or how they would feel against mine.

It was clear I was outnumbered, and digging my

heels in any more would only make me look ridiculous. "I'll see what I can do," I grunted out.

Claudia gave me a thumbs up, then turned away to take a phone call, leaving me face-to-face with Lex. He nodded slowly. "You did a great job today. I'm impressed."

Dammit. My insides went warm, and my stupid pulse picked up speed. All it took was a little praise. *Get it together.* "Are you surprised I know what I'm doing?" I asked with a sweet and completely ingenuine smile.

"Does everything have to be a fight with you?" he asked, keeping his voice low, staring directly at me, and ignoring everyone around us. Was it possible for all of the air to get sucked out of the atmosphere? We were outside, for God's sake, but I could barely breathe.

"Maybe I'm used to feeling like I have to fight," I replied. He frowned but let it go, backing away without another word.

And as usual, I was left feeling like I had just been run over by a speeding train. How did he do that to me?

More importantly, why did I keep letting him?

7

———

LEX

"Thank you so much for this. I know last-minute shit isn't your favorite."

Clay snickered but shrugged it off. "I had the room open tonight. But I wouldn't have gone out of my way to make it available for anybody but you."

"I'm honored." I was also impressed, but then I should've known better. If there was one thing Clay prided himself on, it was the high quality of service his staff offered on every level. He ran a tight ship.

While his restaurants weren't Michelin-star quality, they were just short of it. He always swore he didn't care about earning a star, that it only limited what a restaurateur could do if they wanted to keep it. While he wanted to operate at a high level, he wanted to do it his own way, by his own rules, and not some arbitrary rules made up by a bunch of nameless, faceless strangers.

Now we stood at the bar in the far corner of the small event room off the restaurant's main dining area. He'd opened this West Hollywood location a few months earlier, and all signs pointed to a complete success.

I had entered through a side door but noticed the clamor on the sidewalk and the number of people waiting to get in, even with a reservation. This was where everyone wanted to be seen.

"Here's to you." Clay lifted his glass to me. "Your first day of shooting. How are you feeling about everything?"

How was I feeling? It was easiest to sum everything up in one word. "Exhausted."

He laughed knowingly. "Yeah, it's one thing to watch everything from behind the scenes. It's another when you're the guy everybody is looking at to make decisions."

"Exactly." And when he put it that way, I wanted much more than the scotch in my glass. I downed the rest of it and signaled for a refill while the room started filling up with crew members and cast.

Clay growled when Danica Cole entered, flanked

on either side by supporting actresses whose names I couldn't recall. They were hot, for sure, wearing low-cut dresses, their hair in shining waves, with the same carefully applied makeup and sky-high heels. Did they understand how underwhelming they were when they all looked essentially the same?

It was obvious Clay didn't agree. "I swear, it's not fair," he grumbled, shaking his head. "You have all this fine, fresh pussy walking around all the time, and you can't do anything about it if you want to avoid getting your balls in a legal vice."

That wasn't what I was thinking of as I watched the girls mingling with the rest of the crew, who kept filtering through the door. *Where was Summer? Was she going to show up?*

She probably would, just to prove she had the nerve when it was clear this wasn't her thing. Somebody had to teach that girl the ropes—how to go along and get along. Instead, she went through life with a chip on her shoulder. I didn't think she should be punished for it, but it was clear why people thought she was a pain in the ass.

"Mr. Landry." Danica pretended to notice me for the first time and tossed her hair over one shoulder, strutting my way. It was like the girl glowed as if she had a spotlight trained on her. The golden-blonde hair that had been up in a ponytail during filming today shimmered, and her dress did a lot more for her killer body than the coveralls she'd been wearing earlier.

"Holy shit," Clay whispered, setting his glass down on the bar to turn his full attention to her. "I think I'm about to meet my future first ex-wife."

I barely stifled a laugh before introducing them. "Hi, Danica. Have you met my good friend, Clayton Manning?" I asked, gesturing toward him. I figured it made more sense to introduce them than to go through whatever awkward mating ritual she wanted to enact with me. I knew that look in her eyes—I'd seen it my entire life. If not directed at me then at the powerful men around me with the ability to shape a career or destroy it.

Her smile faltered, but not for long once she connected the name to the man standing in front of her. "Mr. Manning," she purred, extending one slim hand. "What a pleasure. I've been hoping to meet you for a long time."

"I guess it must be fate." He held her hand longer than necessary, staring at her like she was the only woman in the world. It was something he'd polished over the years, drawing a woman in, making her feel special so her panties slid off more easily. He would be thanking me by morning.

For the time being, I was more than happy to quietly make my escape, drifting away to where a group of people were helping themselves to a lavish buffet. "Mr. Landry, this is too much," somebody called out as I approached, but I only shook my head.

"Nothing's too much for you," I insisted. "I'm asking you to do the impossible in no time flat. This is the least I can do to thank you for all the hard work you've already put in. Please, help yourselves. Have a great time. There's an open bar and plenty of food."

Why hadn't she shown up yet? Why did I fucking care? I might as well have been a caged tiger, pacing uncomfortably. Waiting. Watching. Would she skip out? And why did it matter? If she wanted to be miserable, lock herself away, and sacrifice herself for her so-called artistic vision, I should have let her. She was a grown woman and had earned the right to make her life miserable if that was what she wanted.

And then Claudia walked in, and my heart skipped a beat because I knew what that meant. Yet no one followed her. She walked in alone, waved to some of the crew members still loading up plates at the buffet, and raised a hand to say hi to a few actors sitting at one of the handful of tables set up around a dance floor.

I crossed the floor, my eyebrows lifting in a silent question once she caught sight of me.

"There was a little bit of a problem," she whispered when I reached her, turning her back to the rest of the room. When she did, her smile fell away. "Something with one of the permits for tomorrow's shoot. The time was all wrong, and according to it, we're supposed to be shooting at night, not during the day. So now..."

"She has to scramble around and come up with a backup plan," I concluded with a sigh. "Why didn't anybody tell me about this?"

"I'm telling you now." She shrugged helplessly. "I figured I'd come by and let everybody know she's sorry she couldn't make it, but she had to stay home."

Fuck. Not that I was planning on letting loose tonight, but I looked like a prick if I partied with the cast and crew while my director was pulling her hair out, rearranging the shooting schedule to accommodate a clerical error. "Maybe I'll head over to the apartment," I suggested. "I might be able to get on the phone with somebody down at the permit office to get things rearranged. Next time, tell me about it first. I could've saved her a lot of trouble if I had reached somebody during working hours."

"You try telling her that." Claudia rolled her eyes, scoffing, and I found myself liking her a lot. She saw Summer, really saw her, and wasn't afraid to be candid. "You might as well tell a fish to breathe air. She needs to solve everything on her own."

And it would tank this project if she didn't learn to ask for help. "Thanks for the heads up. I'll take care of it." The last thing I saw as I turned to leave was a giggling Danica with her hand on Clay's arm. At least one of us would have a good time tonight. The lucky bastard.

On the way, I made a call. "Marty, you're killing me," I said as soon as my connection at the permit office picked up. Having his personal cell definitely came in handy at times like this.

"What's this about a mix-up tomorrow? You know we need to be out on the track during daylight hours. We're not shooting this scene at night. It won't work."

"I told your girl these things happen sometimes," he muttered, which took me from irritation to flat-out anger. "Sometimes a.m. is put in place of p.m. It was an oversight."

"Is that how they run things down at the permit office? Maybe they need somebody more responsible working in your position."

"Now, wait a second—"

"This is going to be fixed by tomorrow morning," I announced while my driver rounded the corner on Summer's block of Melrose. "My cast and crew are going to show up at that racetrack, and no one will stop them from filming because the permit situation *will* be settled. I don't care what you have to do. Just get it done, or I call your superior and get them to do it for me." I ended the call before he had the chance to give me another bullshit excuse.

By the time my driver pulled up in front of the apartment complex, a text came through.

Marty: *It's taken care of – M.*

I knew better than to ask for an apology for his oversight, choosing instead to step out onto the curb wearing a satisfied smile, scanning the area around me. Three towers surrounded a central pool and patio area where a handful of people swam and listened to music as I walked through. For their sake, I hoped the noise didn't carry too far upstairs, or they might be faced with a screaming Summer.

When I reached her building's lobby, I rang the

bell corresponding to her apartment number. It didn't take long for her to respond. "Yes?"

"It's Santa Claus. I have a present for you."

"Lex?" she asked, groaning. "I do not have time for this. Go party or something."

Unbelievable. I jammed my thumb against the bell again, leaving it there for a slow count of five, then letting go. "Goddammit," she growled through the intercom. "Why won't you take a hint?"

"I'm not fucking around." I sighed. "I'm bringing you something that's going to make your night better. But, by all means, leave me down here while—"

"Jesus! Okay, fine. Whatever." The door buzzed, and I opened it. When I reached her floor, she was waiting with the door open, tapping her foot impatiently.

She looked... *nice*. She had dressed up for the party in a soft, floral print dress. A handful of necklaces in various lengths hung over her chest, and she wore those same silver bangles from our first meeting. They jingled musically with every tap of her foot. "Well? I guess she told you what happened," she muttered darkly.

Right to business, as always, but I swore her eyes dipped down my open shirt for a millisecond before she caught herself. "Claudia? Yes, she told me what's going on."

Her chin jutted out. "She wasn't supposed to send you here."

"She didn't," I replied.

Shrugging, she turned and walked into the apartment. I hadn't been invited, but I took it as a sign I should follow. I closed the door while she crossed the surprisingly spacious living room. The apartment had come furnished, filled with sleek, modern furniture that fit the general vibe I had picked up downstairs.

What drew my attention beyond the increasingly familiar aroma of incense and lavender essential oil were the pages of scheduling strewn across a coffee table like a toddler had come through and torn her binder apart. "I think I have it figured out," she explained. "It'll mean rearranging a chunk of shoots, but we might try to squeeze it in here." She thrust an arm my way, pointing to a date on the calendar she held. "And filming tomorrow's scenes in the morning and then getting down to the pier by early afternoon should work, but only if we really focus and stay on track. I think it's totally doable." She bit her lip hard like she was worried about convincing me.

"You don't have to do any of this," I told her. "It's taken care of. We can go ahead the way we planned."

Her eyelids fluttered, her lips moved, but it took a while for anything to come out. "What do you mean?" She eventually took a breath.

"I got it taken care of. We're still on for tomorrow morning." When she still gaped at me, I asked, "What? Don't you think I can get shit done? Let this be a lesson. Call me in the first place because that's what I'm here for."

What did I expect? Thanks for starters. Maybe a little gratitude. Relief. What I did not expect was her wrinkled nose or the sneer that lifted her upper lip. "Seriously? That's exactly what I didn't want!"

"Excuse me?" I asked. My disbelieving laughter filled the room before I clarified, "You didn't want this to be cleared up with as little trouble as possible? I must be misunderstanding you."

"Dammit! I'm supposed to be the one handling things. Something goes wrong, *I* have to fix it. And I did!" She threw the calendar page onto the table along with the rest, scoffing. "Looks like I wasted my time."

"Yeah, you did," I agreed. She waved a dismissive hand and turned away, walking toward the window. "Don't turn your back on me, Summer," I warned.

Stopping on a dime, she turned around with her mouth hanging open. For once, I surprised her into silence.

"My job is to make your job as easy as I can. Or didn't they teach you that in film school?" I asked. It might have been beneath me, but I enjoyed the way she stiffened. "Get off your goddamn high horse. You wasted hours of your time tonight by insisting on handling something on your own. We are supposed to be working together, aren't we?"

"All I need is for people to start talking about how I have to run to you with every problem I have!" she shouted back, stomping her foot. "I can't have people thinking I'm incapable of doing this job!"

"What the hell are you so afraid of? Why is everything a challenge?"

"Because it just is!" She threw her hands into the air. "Everything! Every day! I thought I finally found a partner I could count on, and what did he do? He used me. He destroyed my reputation, and he's still benefiting from my work. I'm not letting that happen again." Her chest heaved with every ragged breath once she went silent.

"Listen to me." I closed the distance between us, taking her by her bare arms to hold her in place before she could turn her back again. "You have to let the past go. It's getting in your way."

"That is so easy for you to say." Ducking her head wasn't enough to hide her quivering chin. "You don't know. I thought we were building something together. I trusted him. I worked my ass off for him... for us. And he threw it all in my face," she whispered.

Case in point why I never bothered striving for anything long-term with a woman. There were too many expectations involved, along with too much responsibility for someone else's happiness. I couldn't bring myself to get caught up in it, but that didn't mean I agreed with some stupid bastard breaking a woman's heart.

"Fuck him," I spat, though I did it softly. I didn't have it in me to be harsh. Tears were always a weakness of mine, especially when the person shedding them went out of their way to look strong otherwise. "You're going to leave his ass in the dust."

Slowly, she lifted her head, her teary eyes meeting mine before she whispered, "How do I know I won't get burned again?"

"You'll have to trust me." It was a big ask since I could hardly trust myself to stare at her mouth without devouring it. The temptation was almost too much.

"And how do I know I can?"

Damn her for doing this. "There are reasons why I'm not experienced with helping a woman through a tough time, and this is one of them," I gritted out, my grip on her arms tightening. "Why won't you let me comfort you? Why does everything have to be an argument?"

"Nobody asked you to stick around." She glanced down at her arms, then up at me. "Let go of me and get out of here. That'll solve all of your troubles."

"That's where you're wrong." I pulled her close, making her gasp and stiffen. "My troubles started the day you walked into my life, Summer, and I can't shake you. God knows I've tried," I added in a strained whisper.

Her eyes met mine. The pain in them had changed to something else. Something as dark and needful as what blazed its way through me and demanded I lower my head and crush my mouth against hers, turning the undeniable chemistry between us into an all-consuming inferno.

As sweet as I'd imagined. Firm lips parted so easily, willingly, while a faint sigh stirred in her throat, a signal of her giving herself over to me, succumbing the way I did to the heat.

Why bother fighting it? Desire left me pressing my fingers into her flesh, demanding I mark her. Claim her. And every short, needful breath she took told me she wanted the same thing.

My cock surged as she melted against me, her body molding itself to mine while her arms wound around my neck. Tipping my head to the side, I deepened the kiss, exploring her mouth with every stroke of my tongue against hers. My scalp tingled at the touch of her nails, leaving me groaning the way she did while I backed her against the nearest wall and pinned her in place with my body.

Now I could touch her, fondle, caress. Everything I'd held back roared to the surface with almost frightening intensity. Her body was soft but firm, enough to make me want to drop to my knees and worship. I rolled my hips, pressing my painful erection against her hip, savoring her needy moans before doing it again. She would scream for me tonight. She would beg for more.

"Lex..." she breathed out when my mouth left hers to continue its exploration. Her pulse fluttered under my tongue when I swept it over her throat, matching the furious rhythm of my heartbeat. "Oh God, Lex."

I could learn to love the sound of my name tumbling from her swollen lips. "I'm right here," I rasped, grazing her delicate skin with my teeth until she shuddered. Lifting my head, I stared down at her flushed face—eyes closed, lips parted, the very image of abandon.

It was one of those moments that brought a man to a fork in the road. This or that. Take her now, spend the night pleasuring her, and face the consequences tomorrow. Or make the right decision and get the hell out of here before I opened a Pandora's box of fuckery neither of us needed.

Her eyes flew open wide, and a gasp sounded when I backed away, shaking my head. "I shouldn't have," I grunted, dazed and disappointed. No matter how right it felt. How necessary. Even now, watching her smooth her tousled hair, I couldn't regret it. Not when I so desperately wanted more.

There was something much bigger at stake for both of us. The thought softened what was so hard and demanding, pressed against my zipper. I had a job to think about, a studio, and the livelihoods of everyone working there.

Her chest heaving, she nodded, examining the floor as she whispered, "You'd better go."

She was right, no matter how little I wanted to comply. Leaving was the safe option. It was the only option, which I took before I could make another unforgivable mistake.

8

———

SUMMER

"This feels wrong."

Claudia laughed and gave me a playful shove as we walked down Rodeo Drive, window shopping since there was no way on Earth we could afford to buy anything. "Only you can take a day like today and turn it into something negative."

"There's so much work to do. And here I am, strolling around like I'm somebody I'm not."

"What does that even mean?" she asked, lowering her sunglasses so I could see the puzzled look she was wearing. "Somebody you're not. Who do you think you are, anyway? Last I checked, you're making a movie at a major studio, and it's going to be fucking amazing when it's finished. Maybe this is the sort of life you need to get used to living."

The problem was, I couldn't imagine that time ever coming. "You know how it was when I grew up," I pointed out. "All the pressure. All the ideas they shoved into our heads."

"I do know how it was." She wound an arm around mine as we walked. There was something comforting about that. "Your parents were never fair to any of you girls. Their art and whatever. They were too hard on you, and they gave you all these ideas."

"I didn't know you saw it that way."

"How can I not? You're my best friend. I've known you all my life. And they were the ones who gave you all these ideas about your vision and never compromising on it."

"Look at me now," I reminded her. "It must've worked, right?"

"Sure, you'll never be able to enjoy it because you're always going to feel like you should be living in a yurt or something." She shuddered dramatically. "Washing your clothes in a nearby stream or some shit, all because you're a pure artist who doesn't need money. Guess what? The whole world needs it!" She waved an arm overhead, laughing. "I mean, don't pretend this isn't cool… being part of this place. Yeah, a lot of it is fake as hell," she admitted. "But as long as you remember that and you're smart about who you trust, there is no reason you can't enjoy a beautiful life here. Rubbing shoulders with big shots. Getting spa treatments next to last year's Oscar winners and talking about projects you could do together."

Damn, that sounded good, especially the part about networking over spa treatments. It would mean I turned into the snobby elite, the sell-outs. "I'm not supposed to want to do that," I groaned.

"You and I both know you do." We stopped at a red light, and she turned to face me. No more joking, no more smiling. She lifted her sunglasses on top of her head and nestled them in her dark curls. "It's all right to want that. There's nothing wrong with it. You want to make a lot of money. You want to be able to fund your own projects one day. You want to live a comfortable life. That's totally natural."

"I know you're right," I admitted with a sigh.

"And here's the thing, babe. If this movie does well… we both know it will, you're going to be a hot commodity around here. You're gonna be pulled deeper into the machine or whatever you want to call it. And then what?" she asked. "You'll never be able to enjoy it unless you work through this shit now. It'll never be enough. You'll never feel fulfilled because you'll always have guilt over enjoying your success. Put a stop to that shit now before you ruin your life."

"Damn." I was standing on the corner of Rodeo and Santa Monica, fully dressed but completely exposed. She knew me too damn well. "You've been giving this some thought."

"Yeah, you give me a few minutes every day to actually have thoughts." Her laughter rang out over the traffic noise as we crossed the street. "Which is why we both needed a day away from the studio, away from your office, away from everything. If the cast deserves a break, so do you."

"I don't want a break," I grumbled as we walked past a flashy Armani store. "I want to work."

"I swear, you are impossible." She said it with love and maybe a little exasperation.

I lost my breath when a cherry red sports car passed on Rodeo and immediately grabbed my attention. I expected to see a handsome, sharp-jawed man behind the wheel with eyes like black coffee and a smile with the power to turn my knees to jelly.

"It's not him," Claudia whispered, and she was right, but how the hell did she know what I was thinking? My head snapped around so I could gape at her. "Oh, can we drop the crap?" she asked with a sigh. "The sparks have been flying between you two for weeks and weeks. I've lost track of the number of times I almost told you guys to get a room."

It was a good thing I still had an arm linked with hers since I tripped over my feet in shock. "Shut up! No way!"

She gave me an epic eye roll, groaning. "Yes! God, I'm glad I can finally say something. I wanted to all this time, but I didn't want to mess up anything with the movie."

"Wait." I pulled her to a stop in front of Louis Vuitton and let people walk past us in both directions. "I'm being serious. Is it obvious?"

"To me?" she asked with a giggle that didn't make me feel better. "Babe, we've known each other almost our whole lives. I know what it looks like when you're into somebody."

Shit. I was trying so hard to hide it. I barely spoke to him at the studio for fear of somebody seeing or hearing something they shouldn't. It was bad enough that I blushed whenever I noticed him and got tongue-tied whenever our eyes met. No matter how I fought it, there was no forgetting the way he lit me up with his kiss. How natural it seemed in the moment, all swept up in him, to give in to the deep, incessant craving he stirred.

Even now, shaken to my core, there was a flutter in my chest at the memory and much lower too. "This isn't just somebody," I whispered.

"You don't need to tell me that." She was still laughing it off like it was all a big joke, like I had the luxury to take any risks.

"Do you think anybody else has noticed anything? I'm serious."

"How could they? Wait a second." Her narrow eyes and pursed lips told me I was in trouble. "What aren't you telling me? Have you been keeping secrets? We don't keep secrets."

She was right. I went too far with the questions. Now, it was obvious I was hiding something. "Okay. We might have had a moment..."

"What?" Her shriek was loud and shrill enough to grab the attention of people walking past.

My face went hot while I shook my head. "I don't feel like getting into it in the middle of Rodeo Drive."

"Oh my God." She covered her mouth with one hand.

"Claudia, I'm serious. We can talk about it when we get home."

"For fuck's sake, let's go home now!" She was

already halfway to the curb, ready to flag down a cab, when I grabbed her arm.

"I'm dying for caffeine, and there's a Starbucks around the corner." I might have been stalling. The longer we stayed out, the longer it would be before I had to spill my guts. I was going to end up looking like the world's biggest hypocrite for kissing, only stopping when Lex put an end to it, even if it was a one-time thing. Needless to say, I wasn't looking forward to it.

On the other hand, I was tired of keeping secrets. It wasn't so easy to do with Claudia sharing the apartment and the two of us working so closely together every day. It was a minor miracle I hadn't spilled the beans yet.

"Then let's get moving," she urged. How the hell she walked so fast in espadrilles, I had no idea. I only knew we were practically jogging by the time we reached the coffee shop. There were a handful of benches nearby, and I sat on one of them to check my email. She muttered something that sounded like 'workaholic' but went inside to order.

It seemed like I wasn't the only one trying to make the most of a day off since there was hardly anything waiting for me when I opened my inbox. Nothing from Lex. No texts, either. That was a good thing. I knew it was for the best. Nothing mattered more than the movie and then, after that, my career. Getting caught screwing the executive producer wouldn't turn out well for me.

A shadow fell over me, and at first, I thought it was Claudia. That was why I didn't hesitate to look up, shielding my eyes from the relentless midday sun. "You got in and out that fast?" I asked. The question was out before I realized who I was looking at, backlit by the sun but plainly visible. The golden-blond hair and the icy blue eyes that used to intrigue me now looked empty.

My brain didn't want to accept it at first. I had to be imagining this. He'd never, under any circumstances, casually approach me this way. Bile rushed into my throat, and a steady pounding in my head drowned out everything else around me.

"Hey there, stranger," Eric Danvers had the nerve to murmur, wearing an easy grin. "Long time no see."

I had imagined this moment so many times—seeing him again. What I would say, how I would act. I couldn't have predicted how just being in his presence wiped everything out of my mind. There was only one word I could get out. "Eric."

"Were you planning on ignoring me indefinitely? It's a small town, after all."

How did I never see the person he really was? Was it possible I was willfully blind to the real Eric? The man had to be a straight-up sociopath to stand in front of me, smile, and sound friendly after stabbing me in the back.

"Actually, I *was* planning on ignoring you," I told him, then stood and walked away. Claudia had to find me. It wasn't like she couldn't call my cell. She'd understand when I told her. There was no way I would be able to breathe the same air as that man for another minute without clawing his face to pieces.

Of course, he didn't have the decency to let me walk away. "I hear things are going well over at Landry International," he called out, his voice loud enough that he couldn't be more than a few steps behind me. "Come on. We're both making our way out here. Can't we bury the past and move forward as potential colleagues?"

I stopped and turned so suddenly he almost ended up slamming into me. "Colleagues? That's a new one. As for the past, I'd much rather bury you."

He sucked in a breath, teeth clenched in a

grimace. "That's harsh." The worst part? He seemed to mean it. He couldn't. It wasn't possible.

"It's not nearly what you deserve, but we're sort of in public," I spat. "Pretend all you want, but we both know you're riding high on a reputation I built for you. How can you live with yourself? How do you sleep at night?"

His deep sigh came right on cue. "There you go again. Overselling the amount of work you did on the movie."

"I made that movie while you were in the middle of... what did you call it again?" I asked, tipping my head to the side and folding my arms. "Oh, right. A low point. You were feeling full of doubt. Like you were an imposter. Wasn't that the word you used?"

"You know that was a confusing time for me. I can't remember exactly what I said."

"Right, because you were drinking from the moment you regained consciousness until you passed out again," I recalled, nodding. "You cracked under the pressure. No, you crumbled under it, and I picked up the pieces."

His thin mouth went even thinner when he drew his lips together in a smirk. "That was then."

"Right. That was then, when we were working on a small-budget indie movie you were hoping to pedal around the festivals. What's going to happen when the pressure breaks you again?"

He lifted his chin and scoffed, pulling a pair of aviators from where they hung on the collar of his T-shirt. "It won't. I'm in a much better place now." His cold smile paired well with the glasses once he slid them into place.

"For your sake, I hope so because you won't have me around to pick up the pieces this time. And no matter what you believe, I don't actually want you to fail." I waited a split second for relief to touch the corners of his mouth before adding, "I only hope I'm around if and when you do."

He leaned down a few inches, close enough for me to see how his jaw ticked. "Clyde was right about you. You're impossible."

He always knew how to push my buttons. "Fuck you and fuck Clyde," I gritted out.

"I hope the two of you are happy together. You're exactly the same sort of scumbag." I looked past him to find Claudia now on the sidewalk, an iced latte in each hand, her head on a swivel. My salvation.

"Do us both a favor and get out of my face," I concluded, sidestepping him and walking away without looking back. This time, he didn't follow. Probably because he now knew he'd be outnumbered, and judging by the way Claudia's face hardened into pure fury as she stared over my shoulder, things wouldn't have ended well for him.

Her mouth was hanging open by the time I reached her. "Oh, shit. I'm so sorry I wasn't out here with you. Are you okay?"

"Don't worry about it." Sipping the icy drink didn't do much to cool off my insides, but then not much would when the surprise of seeing him was fresh.

"I'm going to take a wild guess that he approached you and not the other way around?" She glanced over my shoulder and sighed with relief. "He got the hint and is rounding the corner. Which reminds me, there was something I've always wanted to ask you."

Maybe the coffee wasn't such a good idea now that my heart was already pounding. "What?" I asked.

"Is it just me, or does he not have an ass?"

I turned my head at the last second and managed not to hit her with the coffee I had to spit out. "Oh no!" She laughed while I choked on my laughter. "I'm sorry! Bad timing."

It was what I needed. To laugh like that, even if I

almost sprayed latte through my nose. "Now that you mention it, his ass is really flat," I agreed.

"Maybe that makes it easier for him to shove his head up there." She waved at an approaching cab. "Come on. Don't think I forgot what you said you'd do when we got home. I need details."

I had dreaded the idea. Now, I was grateful for the distraction. Lex might have been dangerous and all wrong for me, but for today, he was my solace.

9

LEX

It was like I was a kid about to present a project in front of the class—a little sweaty and a lot more nervous than I anticipated. An upset stomach had me reaching for the bottle of Pepto-Bismol within minutes of giving up on sleep and getting out of bed this morning.

For the first time since filming started, Dad and a few of the studio's key executives were scheduled to sit down and watch the rushes. He'd been away the past three weeks of filming, visiting friends on the East Coast, making this his first chance to catch up. I'd been too busy to catch much of the rushes, for that matter, stuck in endless meetings and catch-ups, phone calls, and business dinners. My life had stopped being my own and probably wouldn't be mine again until after the premiere.

I wasn't proud of myself for dissolving into a bundle of nerves like this. If life had given me nothing else, though, it had granted me the ability to walk around like I didn't have a care in the world. My head was high as I strode across the lot, nodding in acknowledgment as various employees waved or called my name. They needed to see confidence and stability. They needed to believe their jobs were secure, something only I could help ensure.

"Everything's almost ready, Mr. Landry," the projectionist told me when I reached the screening room. "Almost everyone is waiting inside."

"Is Summer here?" I asked, hoping like hell she wasn't in there alone with a bunch of old pricks who would smile to her face but disrespect her behind her back.

"I don't think so," he said, ducking into the booth and leaving me outside the door to the room Dad waited to judge what Summer had done so far. Rather than go in, I pulled out my phone to text her.

Me: *Where are you? Screening in a few minutes.*

She wouldn't skip out over us kissing once, would she? It was one thing for us to avoid each other whenever possible over the past three weeks since it seemed safest that way. Less temptation. Was she freaked over the idea of seeing me now along with Dad?

Either way, I anticipated a quick response. What I got was the opening of a door farther down the hall and the appearance of a wide-eyed, pale-faced Summer before she crept out of the restroom.

This was not the girl I expected to see today, the girl who had a way of making my heart jump and my dick twitch every time I set eyes on her. Nerves were one thing, but she looked like she might be coming down with something. "Are you sick?" I asked as she slowly approached.

"Don't worry. It's not catching." She offered a shaky laugh that sounded almost painful and paired well with the strain etched at the corners of her eyes. "Just nerves. Tell anyone, and I'll sneak laxatives into your coffee for a week."

Still with the attitude. Now I saw it for what it was. She put on a good act—confident, ready to give her detractors the middle finger. Inside, it was a different story—something we had in common.

"They're going to love it," I assured her, taking a risk by cupping her shoulders. A brief touch, one I doubted would be misunderstood if anybody saw us.

It was much less than what I wished we could do. I had somehow managed to keep my hands off her since that night at her apartment, and every day, it was a little more challenging to ignore the memories and resist the impulse to go back for more. For instance, the usual parade of women coming on to me at business dinners meant nothing. Not so much as a twitch below the belt. Yet the slightest caress of Summer's shoulders had me surging, yearning to do more. More would never be enough.

Right now, I wasn't thinking about the sensuous, passionate woman. Somebody whose skin, scent, and taste had me yearning for her until I couldn't think straight. Now, I was looking at a nervous, over-whelmed woman who saw her entire future hanging in the balance of what happened today.

Dropping my hands to my sides, I took a deep breath that lifted my shoulders and expanded my chest. "You do it," I ordered, waiting for her to take one deep breath, then a second. Before long, normal color returned to her cheeks. "This is going to be great. Try to have a little faith."

"Faith?" She scoffed gently. "Now I know you're just as worried as I am if you're talking about having faith."

I wouldn't dignify that with a response since it

would start an argument. "Come on," I urged. "Let's get in there and show them what you've done so far." The way she squared her shoulders before nodding stirred fresh respect and made me long to kiss her for luck. Instead, I opened the door for her, and with a ramrod back, she walked inside.

"Here we are," I called out. "I hope everybody's ready to be impressed."

"We were starting to worry about you two," Dad announced with a dry laugh that was completely insincere, at least to my ears. He stood in the middle of the five rows of seats and came down to shake Summer's hand, clapping me on the back after that.

"You know how it is, Dad. Wait an extra few minutes. Keep people hanging. You stir up interest." The handful of stuffed suits in the room laughed indulgently. Even Summer managed to sound sincere when she chuckled. "Now, let's get started. I know you've been eager to see what's been filmed so far."

Rather than sit in the row with Dad and the others, I sat in the back, beneath the window of the projection booth. Summer sat with me, leaving an empty chair between us. Incredible how much I wished she wouldn't, that we could sit together, hold one of the hands she now clasped together in her lap while her breath went short and sharp. As a friend. She needed a friend.

I had to settle for offering a reassuring smile before the lights went down and the screen in front of us brightened. *Here goes nothing.*

The most amazing thing happened. I had already watched some of the footage. Hell, I was there when some of it was shot, but seeing it on the screen in a darkened room allowed me to be caught up in the story. The sweeping exterior shots, the framing, the lighting—every detail had been thought out so carefully, and it allowed the actors to shine.

Actors like Danica, who possessed talent I didn't know existed until now. She was vulnerable, gutsy, and unafraid to look rough and beaten up after a race that went wrong. I was mesmerized by a scene where she dealt with the aftermath of reckless driving that left her best friend in intensive care. Summer had pulled that performance from her.

The screen went bright white once we reached the end of the footage. A moment of silence made my heart lurch sickeningly. The back of Dad's head didn't move.

Summer cleared her throat, and I looked at her, then back at the row of men in front of us. "There you have it," I said, standing slowly. "Now you know what this team has worked their asses off to pull together."

"I'm impressed." Dad stood, which seemed to cue the others into moving like they were first waiting for his reaction. "Really. Fine work, Summer. Kudos to the cast and crew. I look forward to seeing more."

Son of a bitch.

She didn't know what that meant, but I did. Her bright, relieved smile was a bolt of white-hot pain that sliced through my chest. "Thank you," she breathed out, laughing nervously. There was nothing I could do but plaster on a fake smile as she and the executives filed out, murmuring pleasantly. A glance Dad's way was enough to hold me in place, bracing myself.

He was barely able to wait until the door closed before folding his arms and pacing in front of the screen. "Explain something to me," he said, lifting his head and hitting me with a stony stare. "How is it that a woman with a body like Danica Cole is running around this movie in a pair of coveralls?"

More than thirty years of knowing the man, and I still waited for the punchline. I should have known better. He never did have a sense of humor.

"I'm waiting for an explanation," he barked out. We were alone now, meaning he could drop the kindly act. "I thought we understood each other on this. I thought you knew the stakes."

"I do." Rolling my shoulders back, I added, "And what you see up there is the result of that."

"It can't be," he countered, jabbing a finger toward the blank screen. "That is not what we need. Don't tell me you can't comprehend what I'm saying."

"What would you prefer she wear?" It was a stupid question. I knew the answer. I wanted to hear him say it. I wanted him to come out, point blank, and admit what a pandering asshole he was.

"Grow up," he spat. It wasn't the words he used but the way he used them with complete disdain dripping from his voice. "You know what I'm talking about. Short shorts. Low-cut top. A bikini at least once."

"Dad!" Laughing would only piss him off, but that was the only reaction that came to me. "A bikini? The script doesn't call for that."

"Then the script needs to be touched up," he snapped back. "We have to give people what they want, goddammit. Why are you so obtuse about this?"

"This isn't some skin flick where the girl with the big tits bends over a car in a wet T-shirt. This is a real, substantial script." I wasn't getting through to him. What was worse, I wanted to. "Honestly, I'm pleasantly surprised with what Danica has been able to do, given actual material to work with. Don't you see that?"

"Then let her make some shitty art house picture when this is finished." He snarled. "That's none of my business. My business is making money now when we need it most. We don't have the luxury of sitting back and jerking ourselves off, calling ourselves artists. We are in the business of putting asses in seats and collecting the profit. Understood?"

"I think you're underestimating the public."

"I think you're delusional," he countered. "Or is this all some ill-conceived rebellion against me?"

It was almost too pathetic. "Right, because everything's about you," I retorted.

"I can't imagine what else it might be beyond you taking leave of your senses."

Always with an imperious attitude.

Always looking down his nose at me.

"I am making this movie my way."

He looked genuinely disappointed as he sighed.

"Then you are going to be responsible for the death of this studio."

"Don't you put that shit on me," I warned, making his head snap back. It felt good, as if I had finally landed a blow. "This is *your* mess you want *me* to fix. It's not my fault you refused to look farther down the road and see the direction the industry was moving in. Other studios managed to pivot. They ventured into new platforms when you were convinced every new thing that came along was nothing more than a fad. And look at you now," I concluded, scoffing.

His mouth barely moved as he muttered, "Are you finished?" When his voice dropped, that was when he was most dangerous. "Because I have half a mind to fire you."

"Explain that to the world," I pointed out on my way down the row. I'd had enough. If I hung around much longer, I'd end up saying things I couldn't take back. Somehow, in the middle of my almost blinding outrage, I possessed enough sense to put a stop to things.

"Remember what I said," he warned. "I can shelve this movie... take it as a write-off. But if I do, that's going to be the reason I give for the studio's declining numbers. Bad publicity after a failed project."

"No one would believe that."

"Don't you know by now the public believes what we tell them to believe?" The bastard got the last word, beating me out the door. I waited a few seconds, fist clenched at my sides, forcing myself to breathe slowly. Anyone who saw me looking half as murderous as I felt would know something was wrong. We couldn't have rumors flying around.

There was only one place to go. She'd be waiting for me. What was I supposed to say? How could I explain it? We had to find common ground some-how, a way to make everybody happy. The problem was, she didn't give an inch.

There was another problem now. I had seen her work. Rough, unpolished, but damn impressive as it stood and would only get better with editing. It wouldn't be a matter of betraying her, forcing the sort of changes Dad wanted. I'd be betraying everyone in the cast, the crew. Myself. Because I imagined being proud of the finished product if someone gave her the chance.

I braced myself for whatever was about to happen as I stepped into the building across the lot where our offices sat. My door was closed, the room dark, but that wasn't where I was headed. She was in her office, the door ajar like she was expecting me. I tapped on it and eased it open. My heart dropped at the sight of her sitting at her desk, her face in her hands, her shoulders heaving.

I made it a point to close the door before going to her. "What's wrong? Who did you talk to?" Because that was the only reason I could imagine her sobbing like this, almost heartbroken.

She surprised me, though, when she lifted her head and smiled through the tears streaming down her cheeks. "I almost can't stand it," she whispered, taking a breathless little gasp. "I don't know what to do."

"What are you talking about?" I sat on the end of the desk, staring down at her. "What happened? What did I miss?"

"You saw it. You watched it with me. Oh my God!" She jumped up from the chair, clapping her hands together and lacing her fingers on her head. "Lex, it's so good, I can barely breathe. I knew it would be. I saw it all in my head the whole time. But it's... it's special. Isn't it? Tell me I'm not imagining this."

Like I needed things to get worse. "It is special," I murmured, nodding but dying inside. This was all wrong. It shouldn't have mattered so much, seeing her like this—beaming, overjoyed, ready to explode now that she knew she was moving in the right direction and her vision would be fulfilled.

"I mean, holy shit. I can barely breathe. Feel." She reached out and took my hand, placing it on her chest to feel the rapid drumbeat of her heart. "Oh God, I want to start shooting the next scenes. How am I supposed to wait till tomorrow?" she blurted out a high-pitched, almost manic laugh. "This is it. I feel it."

I couldn't tell her. It would only break the heart, pounding like mad under my palm. "I feel it, too," I said, smiling when she did and hating every second.

"Mr. Landry?" A voice rang out in the hall left me pulling my hand back like her skin burned. "Mr. Landry? I saw him come in..."

"In here," I called out, my spirits sinking as Summer's soared. Turning my head toward the door, I added, "Be right with you."

"Let me treat you to dinner," she offered, bubbling over with enthusiasm before pulling herself up short. "Oh. I have work to do tonight. I can order food to the apartment, and Claudia will be out, so we can talk shop without being interrupted. Please, say yes."

Looking into those big, hope-filled eyes, how could I say no?

I couldn't any more than I could keep from hating myself when I nodded my agreement. Tonight. I'd tell her tonight about Dad's caveats, and we'd find a way to work around them.

We had to because I couldn't stand the thought of crushing her.

10

SUMMER

I barely recognized myself.

Flying around the apartment, putting last-minute touches on everything I had arranged. Foil containers sat in a warm oven, sending the aroma of grilled chicken and roasted vegetables wafting my way as I uncorked a bottle of ice-cold chardonnay before adjusting a few of the items on the crudités platter I'd thrown together. The rest of the counter was devoted to plans—my laptop sat open, a revised shooting schedule on display, photos of shooting locations, and various corresponding pages from the script attached to them. I'd made some small tweaks, all of which emerged from the footage I'd seen earlier.

The footage. The rough cut. My whole body

tingled at the memory of viewing it earlier. The thrill. It confirmed what I had known from the beginning—this was a special project, and we had something important on our hands.

My hands trembled a little, running through my hair as I passed a mirror near the front door. Okay, so maybe I had put a little extra effort into my appearance tonight, adding a little makeup, spritzing on a bit of perfume. Not that I was trying to seduce him or anything, but I couldn't seem to shake the impulse to impress him. What was it that had me so conflicted? Yes, I had always wanted him, something that got harder to deny as days turned into weeks, but nothing had changed. All of the reasons for resisting were still firmly in place.

My weakening resolve was the problem.

That and the way my heart leaped when the doorbell rang. I'd texted him earlier, inviting him to come by around eight o'clock. Claudia had left to visit her family a few hours ago, giving me time to get everything set up without being questioned.

Get it together. This is a working dinner. A working dinner I was already starting to regret as anticipation made my pulse race when I opened the door to reveal Lex with a bouquet in hand. "These are for you," he offered with a faint smile, handing the flowers over for me to admire.

"Thank you so much. Come on in." Lord, this was awkward. We were hardly strangers. This was not a date. He hadn't even changed from the crisp shirt and slacks he'd worn earlier today. I needed to get the fluttery feeling out of my system before this went completely off the rails.

"Smells good in here. I hope you didn't go to too much trouble." He said all the right words, but there was something wrong with his tone as he stopped in front of the counter, gazing down at what I'd laid out.

"Everything all right?" I asked as I filled a vase with water and placed the bouquet of daisies, mums, and roses inside.

"Oh, fine." *Right.* That was believable.

With suspicion beginning to build, I replied, "Well, I hope you're hungry. I ordered enough for an army."

"Can we hold off on the food for a second?" he suggested, glancing up from the location photos. "I was hoping we could catch up on some feedback I received today."

Just like that, any appetite I might have possessed

became a thing of the past. "Is that what the flowers are really about? A peace offering?" I asked. I couldn't help the growing dread and what it did to me, stirring disappointment in my heart before he had a chance to say another word. It all made sense now. As happy as I was, I hadn't really noticed earlier, but he looked pretty distraught when he found me in my office.

"Do you always have to jump to that?" he demanded, throwing his hands into the air. "Always so combative. We are on the same side."

"Right, and you're buttering me up, getting me ready for disappointment. I would much rather you just come out with it." Instead of taking the pans from the oven like I had planned, I rounded the counter, facing him with my hands on my hips. "What is it you have to say? Get it over with."

"Don't order me around," he warned, his jaw tightening. "I'm not a member of your crew, remember?"

"Well then, don't treat me like I'm an idiot who can be placated with a bouquet of flowers and dinner."

"*You* invited *me* for dinner!" he reminded me.

Right. I had. "Whatever," I snapped. "Get it over with. I know you've been dying to."

He took in a breath, and I braced myself, waiting

for the inevitable. I should've known this was coming. Yet once his gaze landed on my mouth and stirred a dozen needful thoughts, I found myself trying to remember what we were talking about in the first place. "It's nothing we can't handle," he whispered, his breathing more strained than before, his body almost trembling. With rage? Or something else? "We can work around it. It doesn't have to get in the way of anything."

I had to wonder what he was talking about. The feedback or the energy crackling between us. Why was it always like this? How was I supposed to resist? "Well?" I challenged, breathing hard and trying not to. I had to be strong. I owed it to myself. "Do it, already. Do what you came here to do."

"Don't act like you have the first idea why I came here," he warned with a growl, stepping up close until he loomed over me.

WHEN HIS HANDS landed on my waist and pulled me in, bringing me closer to his intoxicating scent and overwhelming energy, I gave it one last valiant effort. "Let go of me," I muttered, placing my hands against his chest. Meaning to shove until I made contact with his unyielding muscles and forgot everything I thought I knew while his heart beat wildly under my palm.

"I wish I could," he whispered, his gaze focused on my mouth before his eyes met mine. Troubled, burning, the light in them drew me in the way his arms did. "Fuck, I wish I could."

So did I the instant before he crushed his lips to mine, and my resolve shattered.

He parted my lips with his tongue, and I let him. I didn't have it in me to fight what I wanted with every cell in my body. I was too weak. And this was too damn good.

It was so much easier to melt against him, to run my hands up his rock-hard chest and over his bulging shoulders, holding onto them as he claimed my mouth, erasing every last protest in favor of the sheer, sizzling thrill of what exploded between us. He invaded me with his tongue, probing and swirling, exploring while my lips ached from the intensity of his kiss.

And his hands. They were everywhere, stroking my arms with the softest, most tantalizing touch before sliding up until he cupped my face. A whimper stirred in my throat when he broke the kiss and pulled his head back far enough for me to look up into his coffee-colored eyes—so dark, swirling with lust, need, and a hunger that turned my insides to molten lava. "I know what you're going to say," he grunted out, breathing hard. "We shouldn't do this."

Why did he have to say that at a time like this when my clit was throbbing, and every part of me wanted every part of him?

"But dammit," he growled, lifting the fine hairs on my arms and stirring fire in my core, "I've been wanting this too much."

So had I, more than I wanted to admit until now. It didn't matter how hard I fought or how wrong I knew it was. All it took was the slightest kiss for him to set me on fire from head to toe. My body knew a truth my mind didn't want to accept. I needed to hate him because it was safer than craving him.

Nobody needed to know. We could do it once and get it out of our system. This would not be a repeat of my last disaster. *I wouldn't let it.* Whatever I needed to tell myself.

I sighed, leaning in, sinking a hand into his thick, brown hair, pulling him down again. "Don't stop," I whispered into his mouth before electricity ran through me when our lips touched.

The deep growl he let out erased any scrap of resistance I had left. It was a wild sound, the kind that promised a night I'd never forget. His arms closed around my back, and something inside me lit up and took flight, making me wrap my legs around him when he lifted me off my feet. "Bedroom," he grunted between kisses.

I couldn't answer right away. The pressure from his enormous bulge against my pussy made it a challenge to do more than moan. "Second door," I rasped. My mouth moved over his jaw and neck as he carried me down the hall, fingers kneading my ass and making my eyes roll back in my head.

How long had it been since I was touched like this? Obviously, too long since I was a throbbing, breathless mess by the time Lex threw me onto the bed hard enough to make me bounce. I squealed, but the sound was cut off by a gasp when he took my ankles in his hands and pulled me across the mattress.

There was something wild in his eyes. Almost scary. Instead of making me want to pump the brakes, I only craved more, seeing him loom over me as he parted my legs, taking control. I had never met a man who excited me more. Not even close.

He didn't say a word, not that he had to. His hands did the talking—no, playing. He was playing my body the way a maestro played their instrument, sliding up my thighs, pushing my dress higher. The sensations bombarding me were intense enough that I forgot to breathe as I lifted my hips so he could slowly peel away my panties.

This was happening. He was really popping the remaining buttons on his tailored button-down shirt, revealing his perfectly chiseled chest, shoulders, and arms. I reached for him without thinking, needing to touch, indulging as he stretched out on top of me. Every ripple, every bulge, I was going to explore all of him.

His palm cupped my breast, massaging before his thumb circled my nipple through the thin cotton covering it. "No bra," he grunted out, squeezing. I covered his hand with mine and squeezed harder while the nails of my other hand scratched his broad back.

He rolled his hips, and oh God, the pressure from his dick was incredible. My hips moved to meet him, and we both groaned. The sound of his helplessness was a drug, and I needed more.

Sliding a hand between us did the trick. "Summer... oh, f-fuuuck..." He gasped, thrusting against my palm when I found his length. It was so hard and big enough to worry me a little, but I wasn't about to stop this. Not for anything.

His mouth traveled lower over my chest and

down my stomach. When he worked my dress up, I helped him, crossing my arms over myself and pulling it over my head before dropping back again. I was barely on my back, and his hands were on me, taking hold of my breasts so he could lavish long, slow strokes across my nipples with his tongue.

"Mmm... that's... shit. Don't you dare stop," I pleaded because I would die if he did. Every brush of his tongue sent a bolt of electricity straight to my clit, which now throbbed hard enough to hurt. Hooking a leg around him and pulling him in only made it worse. I needed him to touch me *there*.

"Lex... please..." I barely recognized my pitiful whimpering, but it did the trick. All it took was a single finger dragged through my entrance to send me flying over the edge before I knew what was happening. I arched, going stiff in that final heartbeat just as the tension shattered.

The sweetest relief poured over me and rolled through my core. It didn't stop because he didn't stop. "That's it, beautiful. Give me another," he whispered, guiding two thick digits inside me. I was still spasming, and instead of dying down, the sensations went on and on, dragged out with every stroke against my G-spot, heightened the harder he breathed. It was the sexiest sound—deep, guttural, and almost enough to curl my toes.

"Getting tight again," he announced. With his fingers still inside me, he worked his way to his knees to unbuckle his belt with his free hand. "Come for me so I can sink this cock inside this pretty pussy. Do you want that, Summer?"

"Yes!" I sobbed, rolling my hips, working with him. Nothing in the world mattered but this. I needed it to end. The tension was so strong it made me plant my feet on the bed and move my hips frantically up and down. "Please! Let me come!"

It was the thumb he added against my clit that did it. I almost howled when it hit and practically shot me up off the bed. "Yeah, that's right," he urged, working in and out. "Give it to me. Let go."

It's not like I had a choice. I was weak and trembling by the time his fingers slid out of me. Opening my eyes meant watching him watch me. He stared down at my splayed-out body while lowering his zipper, lips parted, chest heaving with every breath.

"I could jerk off just looking at you like this," he said, his voice gritty and heavy with desire. Meeting my gaze, he added, "But that wouldn't be enough fun."

No. It wouldn't. Especially considering the dick

he freed once his pants and boxer briefs were around his thighs—thick and veiny with a wide head. The sight of it made my pussy quiver, and my hand shot out to wrap around his shaft, testing it.

"Fuuuck..." He dragged out the word, letting his head fall back while he thrust his hips. "Shit, that's good." When I propped myself up on my elbow, he buried a hand in my hair and drew me closer.

He didn't need to say the words. I knew what he wanted. After a few experimental licks against his underside, I took his head into my mouth, letting the taste of his precum spread across my tongue, taking more. I was barely two-thirds of the way before he hit the back of my throat, so I used my hand to cover the rest.

"Mmm... that's it... get me good and hard for you..." he whispered, though I couldn't imagine him getting harder than he already was as my head bobbed and his hips moved. Just as I got into a rhythm, he pulled me away with a soft, woeful groan. "Lie back."

That was the most surprising part of all. How good it felt to give up control and follow his commands. I did as he said, working my way back until my head reached the pillows. He pulled a condom from his wallet, tossing his slacks and underwear aside.

Magnificent. That was the only word for his athletic body. My pussy quivered again in anticipation as he positioned himself between my legs, spreading them wider to make room for him. My heart was in my throat. Would I be able to take all of him inside me?

He didn't give me much time to think that over, dragging his head through my slit before pushing forward until I gasped at the pressure that walked the line between pleasure and pain. It lasted only a second. Then, there was nothing but pleasure that only grew bigger the deeper he sank himself.

"You're so fucking tight," he gritted out, grimacing, squeezing his eyes shut. "Gonna make me come, you're so tight."

"You feel so good," I whispered, arching my back, straining for contact with his warm, smooth skin and the flexing muscles under it.

"You think you have another one for me?" he grunted out, moving so slowly I was sure I'd go crazy. No way could I stand much more of this. Sweet torture, feeling every inch of him inside me, stretching and pushing me a little closer to the edge.

I clawed his back and gripped him tight with my

legs, pulling him closer. Who was I? He was turning me into a greedy monster who needed more, all of him. I couldn't get enough of the feeling of his dick stretching me, filling me, moving a little faster with each thrust. Wet noises mixed with the sound of our ragged breathing until bliss pulled me under one last time.

He came with a roar that shook us both. His body went limp against mine for a second before he rolled away and left me aching to have him back. Already, I wanted him back.

But this was already bad enough. I knew it way before the last little tremor raced through my core. There was no time to lie back and bask in the glow when what we did was dangerous for both of us.

He knew it too. "Let me guess what you're thinking," he muttered, eyes closed, stretched out on his back. "We shouldn't have done it and can't ever do it again."

"You know it's the truth," I whispered, half-hearted. Knowing he was right didn't mean I had to like it. Right now, I fucking hated it. I had seen the promised land, as corny as that sounded. How was I supposed to go back to the way things were when I only wanted him but didn't know how it felt to have him inside me?

"I know. And I'm not trying to fuck this up for either of us." He groaned again, sitting up and rubbing his hands over his face. "But don't expect me to forget, Summer."

I watched as he got up, memorizing every detail while he started pulling himself together. "It's for the best," I reminded him.

Maybe I was reminding both of us.

11

LEX

"Thank you very much, gentlemen." I couldn't wait to end the call with the promotions team, who always had an excuse for why shit couldn't get done as quickly as we needed it. There were still participants muttering the usual end-of-meeting crap about circling back and all that, but I couldn't have cared less.

It was better for everyone involved that I disconnected when I did. The posters for the movie were flat, generic, and uninspiring. There was time for revision, but the window was getting smaller every day.

What was it going to take to get everybody on the same page?

I needed a distraction—something to release the

tension. Of course, my thoughts went where they'd been going for weeks. I lost track of how many times I lapsed into daydreams about Summer. Taking her here on my desk in my office. In my pool at home. Bent over the hood of the classic Chevy we were using for the movie—that was one of my favorites, imagining her spread eagle across the hood of that car.

In other words, my right hand was getting a lot of action lately. Even now, I stirred until I had to think of something else, anything to keep from lapsing into another fantasy behind my studio desk.

All it took was thinking about the fact that some unnamed executive had requested something 'slightly provocative' for the movie poster. Who the hell did these people think they were protecting? Like I didn't know exactly who had made that request. They even said the word 'cleavage' had been thrown around. Part of me wondered if Dad wasn't fucking with me, seeing how far I would let him go before I lost my shit.

It might have been better to indulge in the Summer fantasies for a while since I was only getting more pissed off every second. The man had always been a pain in the ass, the micromanaging prick he was.

Always the smartest guy in the room. Never wrong about anything. There was a reason Mom left when I turned sixteen once she was sure I could handle myself without her. I couldn't understand how she stayed as long as she did with a man who would've rather cut out his tongue than admit he made a mistake.

I couldn't decide if this was all because of that tendency or because he had no faith in me. Why bother giving me a movie if he didn't think I could pull it off? It made no goddamn sense, but then nothing about him ever had.

After ten weeks of filming, we had another four to go in principal photography. Then came everything else—reshoots, looping, editing. Sound effects, the addition of a score, and countless other tasks need to be completed in record time if it means having a finished product to advance screen for reviewers. There was also the necessary press junket, something I had a feeling Summer would rather avoid. ~~She'd need help with that.~~

The thought of her made me check the time. I hadn't heard anything about delays on the set today, where the climactic final race was in its last day of filming. The sun was already on the descent, telling me they were losing light and should've been finished by now. Did she decide not to stop at her office before going home?

It was pathetic, but I could've taken that promotions call at home. I didn't have to sit around past seven o'clock on a Friday night. I wanted to because I needed the excuse to see her one more time today.

"Dammit! Would you let me help you?" I didn't recognize the female voice outside my office, but I heard the frustration in it.

"I told you, it's not that bad. The medic said so."

That voice, I knew. Suspicion got me out of my chair in a hurry, and I marched across the room, flinging the door open in time to see Claudia helping Summer limp into her office. "What the hell happened?" I demanded, following them, watching Summer settle painfully into the chair behind her desk.

"It was nothing," she grumbled as she propped her bandaged ankle on the desk. "The damn DP wouldn't position the camera where I wanted it. It wasn't picking up the shot. So I went out to fix it, and I turned my ankle."

"She fell," Claudia almost shouted. There was still an edge of hysteria in her voice, which told me this was more serious than Summer wanted to admit. "She fell onto the damn track and barely rolled out of the way in time to keep from getting run over!"

My heart stopped for one endless, breathless second. "Say that again," I managed to grunt out. "Because I know you did not run out there while the cars were in motion."

She had the nerve to act like she was in the right, puffing out her chest and everything. The wounded party. "We were in a hurry, dammit!"

"We're not in that much of a hurry! I hope like hell you're not putting anybody else in danger with reckless stunts like that."

Her cheeks went red. "Of course not!"

I looked down at her bandaged ankle, shaking my head. It could've been so much worse. Bad enough that the thought turned my blood cold. "What do you think you're doing, taking a risk like that?"

"It's not a big deal. I lost my footing. It happens."

Only Claudia kept me from saying everything that came to mind. Still, I needed a slow, deep breath while they examined scrapes on Summer's palms. "It didn't just happen to anyone," I reminded her. "It happened to you, and it's important you stay alive. Is that too much to ask?"

That wasn't half of what I wanted to say. Blood

rushed in my ears. I was seconds from tearing the room apart. It could've so easily gone the other way. And I'd still be here, sitting at my desk, unaware, thinking about her and wishing she'd come back while there was a chance she ever would.

She lifted her eyes and met mine, but not for long, going back to her scraped hands. "I'll be more careful from now on. Okay? Is that enough?"

"I don't even see why you wanted to come back here." Claudia glared down at Summer and tapped her foot. "I should've taken you back to the apartment no matter what you said."

"I told you I want to check in with the editors. I hurt my ankle. It's not a big deal." I saw another truth in her eyes and had no doubt someone who knew her as well as Claudia did could see the same thing. She was in pain.

"Fine, have it your way." Claudia checked her phone and scowled. "I still wanted to get out to the supermarket to stock the kitchen before I leave."

"Where are you going?" I asked.

"I'm visiting my parents in San Francisco," she explained. "I'll be back Monday afternoon."

"I can send her home in a car," I decided, ignoring the way Summer grunted and huffed in her chair. "And if groceries are a problem, we'll have some sent up. Don't worry. I'll make sure she stays in one piece."

"You don't have to worry about me," she insisted. I ignored her, went to the window, and stared out over the parking lot while Claudia said her goodbyes and left. Once her footsteps faded, I released a long breath.

"Do you think this is a game?" I asked. My voice was trembling, anger bubbling just below the surface. "Or is it that you think you're invincible? Maybe that's the problem."

"I don't need this."

"Maybe you do." I looked down at her in time to see the eye roll and headshake. "You could've gotten yourself killed today. Doesn't that mean anything?"

"I didn't get myself killed, though, did I?" With a grunt, she pushed herself up and out of the chair, then started limping away from the desk. "I have work to do now. If you want to scold me, write up a memo and send it over."

It was the casual sarcasm that did it. A match touched to a powder keg. One that exploded and propelled me across the room. I closed the door before she reached it, then slid an arm around her waist to hold her upright. "Would you stop, already? Look at you. You can barely walk."

"I'm..." She winced, sucking in a pained breath as she tried to shift her weight onto her sore angle.

"Jesus," I growled out. She didn't put up a fight when I picked her up and carried her back to the desk, setting her ass on it. "Now, you listen to me. If you're not going to take care of yourself, I'm going to make sure you do."

"How do you plan to do that?" she asked, jutting her chin out like the defiant brat she was.

The closed door made me bold enough to lean in until her head fell back, eyes wide. My hungry gaze traveled over her face and mouth. The frustration she put me through translated to an even deeper, more primal need. Undeniable, impossible to ignore. "I would chain you to my fucking bed if I had to," I growled out. "I'd follow your every move and never let you out of my sight." I realized I was starting to get hard as the idea took shape in my mind.

Her throat worked as she choked out, "I guess it's a good thing I know how to take care of myself, isn't it?" Her flushed skin told a different story. Those clear, blue eyes drifted down to my mouth before she sighed. "Because that would get very complicated."

It was already complicated, and we both knew it.

With my hands on her bare knees, I eased her legs apart, drawing closer until I was between her thighs. "You're going to have to promise me," I whispered, my pulse picking up speed when her tongue darted over her lips and brought to mind so many ideas for what I would do if I had her all the time, whenever I wanted.

"Promise what?" She gasped when I touched her knees again, inching up the hem of her shorts.

"That I can trust you to take care of yourself." Fuck, this was going too far, somewhere we both knew it shouldn't, but I couldn't stop. Not with my blood humming and my dick straining, and the very real thought that I could have lost this today. I didn't know what it was about her that made me so crazy. I only knew I wasn't ready to lose it.

I took her by the hips and pulled her close, making her gasp when I ground myself against her. "Say it," I whispered, leaning in until her head fell back again. I teased her throat with my lips. She tasted like sweat, sunscreen, and whatever unique flavor that belonged only to her. I could have feasted on her for days, especially when she whimpered so sweetly. "Say I can trust you."

When she didn't answer, I wedged a hand between us, cupping her mound through her shorts and pressing hard. She arched suddenly, almost violently, and started jerking her hips. "Oh my God..." she whispered. "What are you doing to me?"

"I'm reminding you who's in charge around here," I said, rubbing her, ignoring the ache behind my zipper in favor of taking her to the edge. It was my fault for going so long without setting boundaries. Tiptoeing around for the sake of her career when she was careless enough to jeopardize her life. "Say it. Say I can trust you."

Her eyes squeezed shut. "This is... ludicrous..."

"You think so?" My hand went still, and it was no surprise when she groaned.

"No fair," she breathed out, grinding against my hand, desperate for relief.

"I never said I was fair. What's the problem?" I moved my fingertips in slow circles and watched her teeth sink into her lip. "You don't like it? You don't want to come?"

Arching against me, she groaned, "You're a dick."

"I know." I added a little pressure, and her eyes closed again. It was almost too easy. "Give me what I want, and you'll get what you want. Tell me you're not taking any risks, not ever again."

"Fuck..."

"No, that's not it." I pulled back again, chuckling

at her frustration. "You're going to learn. For the rest of this project, you're going to remember your ass belongs to me. You're going to behave yourself. You'll take care of yourself because you owe me a brilliant movie. Got it?"

I pressed harder, taking her to the place where she frantically jerked her hips and chewed her lip to hold back the sounds being pulled out of her. "Tell me," I whispered, my breath coming in gasps as sharp as hers.

"Yes! Yes, yes, I will!" Her legs closed around me, squeezing tight. "Please, let me come!"

"Do it. Come for me." She buried her face in my neck to stifle the sound while her hips jerked. I held her there, one hand on the back of her head, the one between her legs slowing to a stop as she trembled against me. She was totally mine, if only for now.

This wasn't near enough. Not only because I was almost ready to come in my pants. My cock had made me do stupid things before, but I wasn't stupid enough to sink balls deep into my director when there were still people working in the building.

"Claudia is gone for the weekend?" I asked once her breathing slowed. "Then you're staying with me." Her head popped up, but I held it in place, my hand in her hair. "I'm not leaving you home alone to take care of yourself."

"But—"

"But nothing. You said you'd take care of yourself, and this is how you're going to do it. By not being a stubborn brat. If you want to work, you can work from there."

I didn't bother mentioning what else she could do there. I didn't think it needed to be said.

"What are you doing to me?" she asked in a voice full of defeat, eyes darting over my face in a search for answers.

Funny. I wanted to ask her the same thing.

12

SUMMER

Did anybody around the studio know how good Lex was at giving foot rubs?

My cheeks went warm when, as usual, my thoughts wandered back to last weekend. I had spent the ten days since then in a perpetual state of brain fog. Remembering the foot rubs and the times he insisted on carrying me around the house while I pretended to resist being held in his arms or flung over his shoulder. I was stubborn, but I wasn't stupid.

Everything had changed. For me, anyway. I couldn't speak for him, though he did seem sweeter somehow. Kinder. Or was that my warped, hormonal perception screwing with my head? Who could blame me for not being able to think straight after all those orgasms?

How was I supposed to make a movie when I couldn't stop wandering around like a teenager with a crush on the cutest boy in school? Nobody should know, which only made it worse.

And more exciting. I could admit that to myself if to nobody else.

"Do you have a few minutes before you go to set?" All it took was the sound of Lex's voice out in the hallway to make my heart jump. The man only had to exist, and suddenly, everything around me faded into the background. It wasn't fair for one person to be so damn hot, like hot enough to kill my brain cells, because I was smarter than this. Wasn't I?

I sat up straighter at my desk and folded my hands like I was still anywhere close to being a decent professional. If he could keep up the charade, so could I. It wasn't like I had a choice. "So long as it's not too many minutes." Was there anyone out there to overhear me? Was I playing to an empty house?

"That's right," he said as he entered the room. "You have guests coming to visit the set today, right?" He didn't close the door, though he was thinking about it, his hand on the knob, his brows lifting.

"They should get here any minute." Now that we were filming exclusively indoor scenes, we could stay here at the studio and work on the sets for Danica's character's apartment and the garage where she and her friends fixed up their cars. Lex couldn't stop talking about what a relief it was, knowing I'd always be at the studio instead of risking my life out on a racetrack.

He wasn't completely wrong about that. It was a stupid move, even if I would've bitten off my own tongue before admitting it out loud. I wasn't thinking, totally wrapped up in the moment, obsessed with getting the shot I wanted. The ten days between then and now had changed my perception.

And not only when it came to almost getting myself killed, though getting caught with Lex would be another kind of death. The professional kind, the kind I'd have to suffer again and again as I got rejected by one producer after another. Either that, or they'd all want to work with me, figuring I'd fuck them the way I fucked Lex.

Was fucking Lex. Present tense. There was no sense anymore in pretending it wouldn't happen again. We had spent the weekend following my sprain at his house. Then there were the four additional nights I had found an excuse to work late. Not that I needed to lie to Claudia now that she knew the whole story, but still. It didn't feel right to come out and announce I was sneaking off to the boss' house for a little fun when I had been against the idea for so long.

"Just checking in to make sure everything's all right." He rounded my desk but kept a respectable distance for the sake of anyone passing by. "I emailed you a copy of the latest promotional materials."

Right now, all I cared about was the way his cologne made my toes curl. Note to self. *Find out what he uses.* I wanted to buy a little bottle of it to revisit whenever I needed a pick-me-up.

"What are your thoughts about them?" I asked, pulling up the email on my computer. My hands were trembling, not because I was nervous about Mom and Dad visiting, though I was plenty nervous about that, and he knew it, which was probably why he stopped by my office when he had.

That was something I sure as hell hadn't predicted. How understanding he would be once I confessed my nerves about this visit. "*It's always been that way,*" I'd told him while staring out his bedroom window, my half-naked body draped over his. His bare chest rose and fell under my ear, his heart beating in a steady rhythm.

"Nothing else matters but the art. Meanwhile, my sisters and I wore clothes that were so worn out, they were ready to fall off us. I'll never forget the first day of kindergarten when I showed up thinking everybody lived the way I did. I doubt they even wanted to send me to a regular, traditional school. They were probably forced into it."

"What is it your parents do?"

"Mom's a sculptress, though she's dabbled in painting. Dad has an art history degree, and life got better and more normal once he sold out and took a teaching job at UCLA."

"That hardly sounds like selling out," he mused, stroking my back. Every brush of his fingers loosened me up a little more until it felt completely natural to open up and share everything.

"Tell him that," I'd retorted, snickering. *"But unless he's making a living selling his mixed media pieces, he's not a real artist. I know, it's completely screwed up,"* I added when he chuckled.

"I'm not laughing at you," he said with a little squeeze. *"I'm understanding you better. Now I get why you're so damn hell-bent on things always being a certain*

way. How can you help it? They've hammered that shit into your brain your whole life."

"Mom seems enthusiastic enough," I admitted. "But I don't quite believe her. And I know Dad flat-out doesn't approve of me working in Hollywood."

"Your dad doesn't know what he's talking about, then," he decided. "And it's asinine to expect you to limit yourself for some bullshit idea of artistic purity. You can't live up to your potential if you don't have the resources to make the kind of movies you want to make. And you're sure as hell not coasting by. I've never met anybody who works as hard as you do."

"I get the feeling you're only saying that because we're naked in your bed right now."

"It doesn't hurt." He was laughing as he gathered me in his arms while I pretended to fight him for being a smartass.

Two orgasms later, I had to get dressed and leave or else never get any sleep. If there was one thing I needed before an exhausting day with my well-meaning but exhausting parents, it was sleep.

Twelve hours later, here we were, pretending he hadn't spent half of last night with his face between my thighs. It was getting trickier, separating work from my personal life. I wasn't making it any easier on myself by flirting with him in the middle of the day. The problem was I didn't know how to stop. And I didn't want to.

"I'm going to need a little one-on-one time very soon." Glancing toward the open doorway, he leaned in like he was pointing at something on my screen. "What a shame we're going to have all these long days and late nights coming up with nobody around to make me behave myself."

I pretended not to notice the goose bumps that raced down my arms when his breath touched my ear. My nipples went tight, and my pussy moistened. He had basically turned me into Pavlov's dog.

"Keeping both our reputations safe isn't enough to make you behave yourself?" I whispered, frozen still because I didn't trust myself to move. It was too tempting, the idea of leaning in, touching my nose to his neck to inhale his spicy cologne. It took three washings to get the scent out of my hair last night, not that I wanted to. I would've liked to smell it all day. A reminder.

He brushed his fingers over mine, resting on the desk, making a shiver run through me and settle in my core. "I think we're getting pretty good at this sneaking around shit," he whispered, caressing the inside of my wrist because he knew it drove me crazy. I squirmed a little and squeezed my thighs together, but it was pointless trying to ease the ache he started up.

"Right, but let's not push our luck." A girl walked by carrying a stack of scripts, and I cleared my throat. "Let's look at this promotional stuff."

Before we could do that, the phone on my desk rang. It was more effective than a bucket of ice water over my head, making me completely forget whatever tingling was going on between my legs. Now, my heart was racing for a different reason, and it brought a little bit of nausea with it. I knew what the call was about before I picked up the phone.

"There's a couple out here saying they've come to see you," the front gate guard told me. "Doug and Brenda Strawbridge."

"I'll be right down to meet them." I blew out a long breath as I hung up the receiver.

"Hey." Lex's hand touched my back, which I wished released the tension that had my muscles all locked up. Even he, with his magic hands, didn't have the power to do that. "You know, if this has you stressed, they don't have to come on set. I can go out there and make a big thing about keeping the public away while we're filming. I'll be the bad guy."

I couldn't have imagined laughing while feeling this way, which meant the laugh that burst out of me came as a complete surprise. "I don't think you need to do that." I giggled. "Thank you."

I looked up at him, his eyes meeting mine. He was smiling, his eyes twinkling, and something dangerously close to real feelings swelled in my chest. I couldn't let that happen. I would have to nip it in the bud. But for now, it felt pretty good. He was the comfort I needed when I felt weak and unsure of myself.

"You said your mom is pretty supportive about this, right?" he reminded me.

"Yeah, but Dad has been mysteriously busy every time we get on the phone." I worried as I stood. Running my hands down the front of my soft, flowing linen dress, I asked, "Do I look all right?"

"That dress looks nice on you." He lowered his voice, glancing at the open door, adding, "But it would look a lot nicer on my floor."

"I can only handle one complication at a time, Mr. Landry." And he was definitely a complication, though a much more pleasant one than the one I was currently on my way out to meet at the front gate.

I couldn't afford to think that way, either. He was extremely dangerous, no matter how good we were together. That wasn't enough to outweigh the damage he could do. Even if he didn't mean to, and at this point, I knew he wouldn't mean to get in the way of my chances at a career. He could still do it without meaning to.

"You don't have to come with me," I whispered when it was obvious he was not going to hang back.

"I want to get a look at them. And they are going to visit my set," he added in a deeper, more serious voice that reminded me a lot of his father, something I knew better than to say out loud. We both had issues with our parents and the bullshit pressure they'd put on us.

"Try not to get offended," I warned as we approached the gate. It was surreal, the sort of moment that forced me to take a step back from myself to appreciate it. I was welcoming my parents into the studio where I worked. I was showing them around for them to see what I did every day. This was my life. I had a right to be proud of it.

That pride lasted around three seconds then I caught sight of Dad looking around like he was already counting the seconds until he could leave. His body language screamed discomfort with his shoulders up around his ears and his arms folded. My stomach churned at the way he peered at everything from over the wire rims of his glasses. Judging it all.

Mom noticed me first and fluttered my way in a flurry of bracelets and fringe. "There's my filmmaker!" She was thrilled, pulling me in for a tight hug. Why couldn't it always be like this? I could bask in the warmth of her love and approval and breathe in the familiar blend of scents that was uniquely hers—incense, essential oils, sunshine. I didn't know sunshine had a smell until now.

"Hi, Daddy." I stood on tiptoe to give him a peck on his bearded cheek. "Thank you for coming down like this. Did you find the hotel all right?"

"Hotel..." he scoffed. "We didn't need anything more than a bed and a decent continental breakfast."

"And we got both," Mom concluded, rolling her eyes as she patted his chest. "Don't listen to him. It was wonderful of you to reserve such a nice room for us."

"Shouldn't you be saving your money?" Dad asked. "For after this is over? You'll need to support yourself between projects."

"I'm fine." And embarrassed. So very embarrassed. Namely because neither of them had acknowledged the man standing just behind me, who until now had been silent.

He cleared his throat, briefly touching a hand to my lower back before speaking. "Mr. and Mrs. Strawbridge, it's a pleasure to meet you both. I understand we have you to thank for Summer's work ethic. It is definitely coming in handy around here."

I could've kissed him. "Mom, Dad, this is Lex Landry," I said. "He's the executive producer on the movie."

"Of course, Mr. Landry." Mom shook his hand warmly. "It's a pleasure to meet you. Summer has said nothing but positive things about this experience."

"Has she?" He laughed softly, smirking at me, asking, "Did you tell her to say that?" We laughed together, and now I wanted to kiss his face off. Mom always was a sucker for flattery and banter with a handsome man.

Dad didn't find it so funny. "Exactly how many people do you employ here, Mr. Landry?" he asked, observing a handful of people walking past. "It seems like a pretty big place."

"I don't have exact numbers on hand," Lex admitted as we started strolling down the wide span between soundstages once we passed the offices.

"But Landry International employs hundreds of people. Of course, there are people who work behind the scenes on every film... electricians, sound artists, props, sets and costumes, hair and makeup, visual effects. But there are also accountants, administrators, our promotions department, and many more positions that are all filled in-house. It's a small city," he concluded.

It wasn't so much the way he rattled off an answer like that. It was his enthusiasm. The way he acknowledged people as they crossed our path. That special touch he had. Whether he wanted to admit it or not, he liked working here. He was proud of the work he did.

"That's really fascinating," Mom offered. I had to give her credit for trying. She understood something Dad didn't—how the situation with Eric wrecked me. She knew having me work here at Landry International was a hell of a lot better than the brokenhearted, directionless depression that had almost won out in the month after the breakup. Culminating, of course, with the award at Cannes— an award I should have been there to accept.

My father, on the other hand, possessed no such understanding. "And if a movie doesn't do well, what happens to all these people with their jobs on the line?" he asked as we entered the dark, cool sound-stage where I'd be working today.

"Now you're asking me to reveal special, insider knowledge," Lex joked. Mom laughed, and so did I, but it was strained and false. "Trust me. We've had more than our share of flops over the years, just like any other studio. We are a well-oiled machine, I assure you."

Something about the way he said it made me stop short, looking up at him. For some reason, I had the feeling that it was the first lie he had told since introducing himself.

"I have an idea." Lex pointed to an area near the craft service tables, where chairs sat. "Why don't we head over there while Summer gets everything ready? I'd be happy to answer any questions you have about anything you see or hear. Making movies is my favorite subject."

Not even my father was capable of breaking through that wall of charm. He followed Mom and Lex over to the coffee station, where Mom burst out laughing and swatted at Lex over something he said. She actually swatted playfully at him.

"I know I'm imagining this." Claudia's sudden appearance at my side startled me, but she was too busy gaping to apologize. "Is your mom literally swooning over Lex Landry right now?"

That wasn't what kept me staring after them.

He didn't have to do this. He probably had six more important things to take care of.

Instead, he was taking care of me by taking care of them.

If I wasn't careful, I might end up falling in love.

13

LEX

"All in all, it wasn't too bad, spending most of today with them. It was a hell of a lot more interesting than sitting behind my desk all day," I concluded, finishing my scotch.

Travis smirked at Clay, then turned that smirk on me. "Look at you. Busting your ass to impress Mom and Dad."

"Fuck off," I growled out. Why did I bother opening up? Busting balls was one thing I had always enjoyed, but there were times when it wasn't called for.

"Lay off him." Spencer laughed. "He had a long day appeasing the hippies... I mean, artists."

"You can fuck off too," I invited, giving him a dirty look that got everyone laughing again.

"How's Danica?" Clay asked me, grinning.

"Wow. I'm surprised you remember her name," I replied. It wasn't bad, giving back a little of the shit I had just received.

"Some women are worth remembering, especially extremely flexible women with D-cup tits and no gag reflex." His gaze went soft and kind of hazy like he was letting himself indulge in memories.

It didn't help that he mentioned the word flexible since that word described Summer well. It took nothing to get me thinking about her, missing her body. She had sunk her claws into my mind and refused to let go. Or was it my balls? Either way, I couldn't stop wanting her.

That very minute, sitting with my friends in a familiar bar, I wondered how she was doing. She and Claudia were supposed to have dinner with the Strawbridges tonight. Did her parents have any questions about me after the hours I spent with them?

No one asked me to. No one had to. Frankly, I hadn't planned on it. Once shooting started, I was gripped, fascinated by what went on behind and in front of the camera.

And I wasn't alone. Even that irritating, self-important father of hers had managed to shut the hell up during the scene where Danica had it out with her ex, the older brother of her best friend, who at that point in the movie was hospitalized after an accident during a race. His character was scared for his sister and furious with the woman he loved but also worried for her, seeing in full color how dangerous their world could be.

Meanwhile, Danica's character helped me understand why the script meant as much as it did to Summer. They might as well have been the same person at that point in the film, where she struggled to find a balance between her passion and the life she lived around it. As much as she cared for the people who mattered, she was almost fanatically devoted to her passion for racing.

Substitute filmmaking for racing, and I could have been describing Summer herself—single-minded and laser-focused, even if it meant driving people away.

"I assume we all have tickets to the premier," Travis called out to me.

Nodding, I replied, "Oh, sure. I'd love to have you guys there, you know that. But there's still time between now and then to get that shit settled."

"Not much time," Spencer reminded me. For some reason, he thought I'd forgotten or had lost track of the days. "It'll be here before you know it. What do you think happens after that?"

"Oh, fuck me," I groaned out. "Let me get through this first, I beg you."

"Are you going to give her one of those deals like what's his face over at Sunrise?" Travis asked. "The guy you were originally thinking about working with?" It was completely innocent, but it left me glaring at him until he cringed. "What did I say? It was just a question." I watched as he looked at the others, hoping for backup.

"What's up your ass?" Clay asked.

I didn't like the concerned look he wore. "It's a sore subject," I explained to Travis. "Turns out I dodged a bullet, missing out on working with him. As for a deal... I'm not sure," I admitted. The idea had blown through my mind, but I never stopped to give it much thought. Not seriously.

I couldn't voice the truth. I couldn't force myself to say it out loud. It wasn't my call. Not completely. Dad had to give final approval on any sort of long-term deal. Considering Summer was only supposed to be the inclusivity hire, it didn't seem likely he'd want to keep her on. Considering I hadn't tried for a second to make the changes he wanted to the movie, I doubted he'd feel charitable when all was said and done.

But he would get over it because he would see I was right. The public would back me up on this. I'd never been so sure of anything in my life.

Travis went outside to check in with the nanny on a call while Clay went to the bar to order another round. Spencer took the opportunity to pull out his phone, and the way he smiled at the screen told me Rowan had texted him. It transformed his face. He looked peaceful.

It was a relief to have an excuse to check for any messages from Summer. I had been wanting to ever since I sat down, telling myself to get a grip. I wouldn't act like a lovesick puppy. I was Lex-fucking-Landry, and I had never chased after a woman in my life.

Still, after she'd spent hours with her parents, it seemed reasonable to check in and make sure nobody was dead. I figured she'd see it once she got home.

Me: *Hope you're enjoying dinner. Talked you up all day. They seem nice.*

All right, maybe the last part was an exaggeration. Her mother seemed all right—a little over-the-top and heavy on the patchouli for my taste. But even after everything Summer told me their bullshit ideas about art, she was surprisingly interested and enthusiastic, peppering me with questions between takes and listening intently to the answers.

Her husband, on the other hand? There had never been a person born who would tell him a damn thing. In other words, he was just like his daughter but without the qualities I enjoyed.

By the time Clay rejoined us, I received a response. Was I smiling the way Spencer had? There was no reason for it. We didn't have what he and Rowan did.

Summer: *Need to see you tonight. Important. Your house?*

It was amazing how my head could buzz with questions at the same time my dick began to swell. There was nothing I wanted more than to see her tonight, and I had only spent last night with her. There was no such thing as enough, and I never slept as well as I did after we spent the night together.

"I swear, it'll be a miracle if I can find a nanny who lasts more than a week," Travis grumbled as he dropped into his seat. Noticing me, he asked, "What are you grinning about?"

I finished sending my reply to Summer. "I was thinking about how well I'm going to sleep tonight."

SHE WAS WAITING in her car when I arrived, parked at the bottom of my driveway. At my approach, she flipped on her headlights, following me up the winding drive until we reached my front courtyard. This had to be serious. Why else would she sit there like that, waiting like some starstruck fan hoping to meet their idol?

She climbed out of her car and slung her purse over her shoulder before marching straight toward me without saying a word. "What happened?" I asked as she approached. "Did something go wrong?"

There was only time for her to shake her head slightly before she launched herself at me, throwing her arms around my neck and burying her face against my shoulder. "Thank you. Thank you a hundred million times."

The last thing I expected was the one thing I needed. "What did I do?" I asked, wrapping my arms around her waist to hold her closer. Something about holding her, even like this, totally innocent, soothed me. It softened part of me I didn't know was there until I met her.

"Are you kidding?" She laughed softly as I set her back down on her feet. Her eyes shone in the moonlight, sparkling, almost hypnotizing me. "You wowed them! Even Dad. I had to pinch myself."

"What did they say?" With an arm around her shoulders, I led the way into the house. She came along without saying a word, neither of us confirming she would be staying. I knew she would without asking. I had her again tonight, and she wasn't going anywhere until I said so.

"Mom actually said she had no idea there was so much that went into making a movie. Can you fucking believe that?" She threw back her head and almost shouted with laughter once we were inside, walking to the living room. She was practically bouncing on the balls of her feet, overflowing with excitement and probably a lot of relief. "All these years, I've been making movies, and now they bother to pay attention to how complicated it is."

I easily imagined her interpreting the situation in a very different way, which made her positive attitude that much nicer to hear. "What did your dad say? He's a tough nut to crack." That was the kindest way to put it.

"He's impressed with how much you know about the project." She flopped down on the sofa and kicked off her sandals, tucking her feet under her. "He didn't expect somebody in your position to know the first thing about the details because, of course, you're only supposed to care about the money."

When she looked down at her lap, I didn't bother stifling my laughter. Dropping down next to her, I asked, "Oh, you mean the exact thing you accused me of?"

"I guess I walked into that one." She shifted her weight until she was on her knees, then threw one leg over me. She hiked her dress around her waist before settling in, then draped her arms around my neck. I liked the direction her mind was going in. "The only thing I've been able to concentrate on all night is how I was going to possibly repay you for doing me that huge favor today."

Sometimes, it was like the woman read my mind. If there was anywhere I needed her, it was like this, wiggling in my lap with the heat from her pussy soaking through my slacks and her tits in my face, so firm and full, her nipples tightening against the soft fabric covering them.

If there was one thing I appreciated about her free-spirit attitude, it was her hatred for bras.

When she reached up to release the clip that held her auburn locks in place, I watched with bated breath as she shook the twist free. A waterfall of soft sweetness cascaded around me as she leaned down and pressed her mouth against mine.

That was all it took. My desire for her flared to life, bursting into flames and threatening to consume us. My fingers curled, digging into her ass cheeks before I pulled her down tight against my dick. Her throaty moan was all I needed to do it again, pulling her tight against me, and we moaned when she started to grind.

"Remind me to invite your parents to the set all the time," I grunted out, kissing my way down her throat, finally probing my tongue deep between her heaving tits. She slid the dress straps down over her shoulders, and I did the rest, tugging down on the fabric until her tits tumbled free. Perfect, luscious tits with rosy nipples that begged to be sucked. I took one between my lips, and she ground harder, faster, her fingers running through my hair until my nerves hummed and precum soaked into my boxer briefs.

"Please, d-don't stop," she begged. "Harder... s-suck harder. God, you're so good..."

So was she, and we were better together. I panted like a mindless animal, caring about nothing but *more*. More to feel, more to taste, more of those sweet, sensual moans.

"I need you inside me," she whispered, throwing her head back and filling the room with the sounds of her pleasure. It was something I wanted to hear for the rest of the night until we passed out.

I settled for lifting her off my lap long enough to pull out my wallet and unzip my fly. She didn't bother getting rid of her thong, so impatient, desperate for cock, that she pulled the crotch aside once I had the condom in place. She reached down and guided me inside her tight, hot sheath, and I watched, fascinated, as I disappeared inside her.

"Fuck!" she shouted, slamming down to my base. I'd never get tired of the first moment when she gripped me when I was fully inside her, watching the way her face worked, and she bit her lip as she started to move. Her eyes drifted shut as she gave herself over to pleasure. She took it as seriously as she took everything else, giving it her all.

I was the lucky son of a bitch who got to witness it, to feel her grip me a little tighter with every downward stroke. I pulled her dress over her head and feasted on her again, delivering one kiss after another, covering every inch of skin within my reach and claiming it as my own. Marking her with every scrape of my teeth, every swipe of my tongue.

"Lex... oh, shit, Lex..." She whimpered, and I tipped my head back, looking up at her, surrounded by a waterfall of auburn silk. The scent of her arousal and the sweat that began to flow from her pores was sweeter than any perfume. I wanted it on me, all over me.

I nipped her mouth, brushing my tongue over her lips. "Are you gonna come for me? Squeezing my cock with that tight pussy..."

"Yes!" She shuddered, slamming down again, losing her rhythm.

"Say it," I whispered into her mouth, stroking her tongue with mine. *"I'm going to come for you, Lex. You're going to make me come."*

"Oh, Lex!" she moaned out. "I... I'm going to come for you! Oh, God, you're going to make me come!"

I was there with her when she tightened a little more with every word she shouted. Her pussy squeezed my length until my balls lifted, and the tingling at the base of my spine signaled the end coming. "Soak my cock," I demanded, pulling her down faster, harder, until she shrieked.

Her release was so sweet. I closed my eyes and let go, let her milk me, let her drain my balls while she whimpered in my arms. "And that was my way of saying thank you for today," she whispered in my ear, still breathless, still trembling. "You saved me."

"I don't know." I eased her off my lap to get myself cleaned up. "I think I'm going to need a little more gratitude. Upstairs in the shower, if that's all right with you."

"Now that you mention it..." She stood on shaky legs but pulled herself together, grabbing her dress and throwing it over her shoulder before treating me to the sight of her exquisite ass as she sauntered toward the stairs. "I'm feeling a little dirty."

14

SUMMER

"I just want you all to know how happy I've been working with you." Looking around the set, I could barely hold back the emotion swelling in my chest. It made my throat tight and my eyes sting with tears, which I fought to hold back.

This was the last day we'd work with the entire main cast. I didn't think it would hit me this hard until I was a few minutes away from calling action on our first take of the morning. Danica trotted over to me with her arms outstretched, and one by one, everyone else followed until we were clumped together in one huge group hug.

"Come on," I continued, laughing a little the way

everybody else did. It was time to pump the brakes before we all got emotional. "Places in five."

Claudia brought me a bottle of water once I was no longer surrounded by the cast. "That was really sweet," she murmured.

"I didn't expect that," I whispered back. "I'm really going to miss this. It just, like, slammed into me when I wasn't paying attention. I'm going to miss these people."

"This movie means a lot. You never forget your first time, right?" She winked, then sat down with her phone. "By the way, they just sent the finalized promotional stuff via email."

"You look at it for me," I decided, then, of course, immediately pulled out my own phone because I couldn't wait. But before I could open my email, a text from Lex caught my attention.

Lex: *Found this under my pillow this morning.*

Attached to the message was a photo of a pale blue thong hanging from Lex's finger. Looking at the background, it was obvious he took it while in his office. My heart seized for a split second, but I reminded myself there was no way anybody could ever tell it was mine, for one thing. And for another, I doubted he was swinging it around his head, running up and down the hallway.

"Oh, you like it?"

Claudia's question made me pull my phone against my chest like I was hiding something. "What?"

Her nose wrinkled. "The posters? I thought that's why you were smiling."

Right. Because that's what I was supposed to be doing, Checking out the attachments on that email. "Oh. No. I got sidetracked."

She slowly arched an eyebrow, eyes narrowing, lips pursing. "Careful." That was the only thing she said, but it was more than enough. I got the message.

And I was annoyed with myself that she even had to say it. I had no business flirting with the boss in the first place, but especially not while on set. He could send me a message like that, but it didn't mean I needed to engage. The man was too tempting. He had the power to make me forget everything I cared about.

"Okay, everybody!" I took a seat in my chair behind the monitor. "Let's have places." Because I was here to do a job.

One thing was for sure. There was no distracting me while I was filming. Lex could have walked on set completely naked, and I might not have noticed. Could this be my life? Yes, I always planned on making movies. I had known that from childhood, making movies using an old camcorder somebody was going to throw out.

But could I do it here? Or somewhere like here, anyway. Once the movie was finished and took the world by storm because it would, I knew it in my soul—what happened next? If there was one thing I had learned, it was how much nicer it was to create art when there were resources available. Dad would've had a field day if he ever heard me say something like that, but it was true. Sure, magic could be created on a shoestring, but it was a hell of a lot more fun if the shoestring was a little thicker and longer.

Was it dangerous to imagine keeping my office at the studio? Not because I thought Lex owed me anything, or I expected preferential treatment since we were sleeping together, but because I was good. I did good work for him, and we worked well together, bizarrely enough. Even our disagreements were fun. My pulse picked up speed at the thought.

Would that be enough to build a future on, though? I wasn't sure I could go back to shoestring budgets now that a major studio budget had spoiled me.

At noon, I called lunch, then chatted with electricians as they repositioned the lights for the afternoon shoot. All of them had been around the studio for years, decades in some cases. They were like a family, joking, laughing, and working together like they had been at it all their lives.

"Have you always worked here at Landry International?" I asked one of them, a man in his fifties with what could only be described as a glorious mane of silver hair, which he wore in a ponytail when he was working.

"Shit, no," he drawled, grinning. "Don't get me wrong. I'm always up for another project here. I've been all over the place."

"What was your favorite job?"

"Oh, I lit the Oscars for a few years." He scratched the top of his head, then rested his hands on his hips as he thought about it. "I've done sports events all over the country. And if you're lucky, you work with a lot of the same people. You get recommended for stuff, you recommend your friends. It's like a whole family helping each other out."

It was corny of me, but the word 'family' brought me that same warm, chest-swelling feeling. There was nothing like the feeling of working together on a common goal, understanding each other, or pushing

each other to work harder. There were no guarantees in this business. I had no idea if I would ever
work again, and the thought was terrifying if I let
myself sit with it long enough. Would I ever find this
again? Or was this lightning in a bottle a one-time
thing?

I headed over to grab myself something to eat
from the craft service table, but Claudia intercepted
me before I could fill a plate with kale salad. "Can I
talk to you for a second?" she whispered, standing
practically on top of me.

"You look like you saw a ghost." And my stomach
was growling, which was why I reached for a pair of
tongs in the big salad bowl.

She took hold of my wrist and shook her head.
"Not exactly, but I did see something you need to
know about. Just come here."

I let her pull me aside, looking around like she
was afraid of being noticed. Right away, my thoughts
went to Eric. What did he do now? Did he already
have a star on the Walk of Fame?

"Don't freak out." She watched over my shoulder,
nervous, while handing me her phone. "I'm sure it's
nothing."

Nothing that looked a lot like photos of Lex and

Danica flirting on the lot. "Does Danica have what it takes to tame the playboy?" I whispered, reading the caption beneath the photos. Somebody took them from outside the studio gates, some paparazzi looking for an excuse to start a rumor.

Whoever they were, they had found it. In the photos, Danica was laughing, touching his arm, and at one point, they leaned in like they were sharing a joke. They weren't even all that close together, but whoever took the pictures and sold them to the highest bidder definitely wanted it to look that way.

"That's fine," I said, handing the phone back. But was it? Why was my heart racing? It was a stupid, lazy attempt at stirring up drama. It didn't mean anything.

And even if it did, I had no right to get upset. That was what happened during casual flings, which Lex and I definitely were. There was nothing serious going on. We were having a good time. He wouldn't be the first producer to hit on an actress.

But he didn't. I couldn't believe he would, and not out of any loyalty to me. That wasn't how he operated.

"Are you okay?" Claudia asked.

"I'm fine. Really." So long as I could keep myself from thinking too much about Eric. This wasn't the same thing, not even close. Not only had Eric liter-ally screwed around on me—more than once, as I found out—we were an actual couple at the time. Committed. At least, I was.

"Do you think she knows about it yet?" Claudia jerked her chin slightly. I didn't have to look behind me to know she was talking about my lead actress.

"I'm sure her agent told her all about it by now."

"It's probably nothing," she insisted.

When was she going to stop trying to comfort me? "Babe, I'm serious. It's fine."

I was grateful my phone buzzed with a call. Instead of letting her answer it, I did once I saw who was calling. He would want to talk to me, after all.

The second I answered, Lex blurted out, "It's nothing. I have no idea what this is supposed to be about."

I tried to ignore my relief as I walked the set, adjusting props for lack of anything better to do with my hands and the anxious energy flowing through them. Why was I anxious? I knew he was telling the truth. It was the way he called me immediately that lessened the tension and eased the ache in my heart. "Hey, there's no such thing as bad publicity, right?" I asked with an empty laugh as I watched the cast and crew wrap up their lunch break.

"Only if it's not a bunch of blatantly made-up bullshit. Which it is. I don't know who the hell these assholes think they are, but they're gonna get a call from our legal department." I saw him in my head, pacing his office only yards from where I stood on the soundstage.

Was he sincere? Or was he going overboard trying to prove his innocence? Usually when people did that, they were guilty.

"It's not all that harmful, though, is it?" I pointed out. "Not that I'm trying to tell you what to do or anything. Whatever you think has to be done."

He paused for a long beat. "You sure you're all right? You seem detached."

"Honestly, there's a lot to finish today, and I'm a little overwhelmed." That sounded true enough.

He was right. I was detached. There was nothing to attach myself to. We weren't together. We were not a couple. The world would never know about us.

But dammit, it would be too easy for everybody to find out, wouldn't it? That was the problem. There were people outside those gates all the time, sometimes blending in with the rest of the world, sometimes not, always looking to get an edge on their competition. To sell a great photo that would grab attention and spark theories and gossip.

It'd be so easy for that photo to include me unless I was extremely careful. All it would take was getting a little too close to Lex in public, and all of a sudden, I would be in the middle of a love triangle. Something twisted like that.

At the end of the day, this film would eventually wrap, and I'd have to continue with my life. There were no guarantees.

"A long day deserves a little fun in the evening." Right on schedule, Lex's voice deepened, heavy with intimacy. "How about you go for a long swim in my pool before I treat you to a massage?"

That sounded nice. Too nice. And it would've felt so good to give in because, in the end, that was exactly what I wanted—a night with him, just the two of us. The rest of the world could be left behind for a little while. I didn't have much more time with him.

But it would always be this way, even if we decided to give 'us' a try for real. The paparazzi would always be just outside the gate, waiting for one of us to take the wrong step. Because Danica and Lex weren't actual people to the public. They were fodder, a commodity.

And there I was, hoping to make a name for myself in the same town.

"You know what? I think tonight is girls' night." Lowering my voice like I was telling a secret, I added, "I haven't been spending a lot of time with Claudia lately. I think she's a little lonely."

Was that true? Not really. I did feel like I was neglecting our friendship a little, but she was making friends and going out sometimes to dinners or clubs. She wasn't sitting around waiting for me to give her something to do in her downtime.

But I had already gone too far with him. It was obvious. That stab of pain when I saw them together in that photo made everything clear. I had to start thinking for myself again, which meant ignoring my body's needs for a little while, no matter how demanding it was.

"Are you sure you're not pissed?" he asked.

"Why would I be? Like you said, it was nothing. Besides, I wouldn't have any right to get all up in my feelings."

Silence. The kind that only lasted a second or two but felt much, much longer. "Yeah. I see what you mean. I hope the afternoon goes well."

"Thanks." That wasn't the most awkward conversation in history or anything. It definitely wasn't the most satisfying. I had no right to expect him to give me the answer I now knew I wanted. That I would have a reason to be hurt or offended if he was screwing around with Danica or any other woman.

A girls' night was definitely what the doctor ordered. The more time I spent away from Lex, the safer I'd be.

15

———

LEX

The son of a bitch.

The stupid, pedestrian son of a bitch.

I had seen him pull this shit more times than I could count, but he had never done it to me. Dad was never stupid enough to pull me into his schemes for free publicity. Whenever he thought a project wasn't going to make bank, he would arrange something with one of his favorite sleezebag photographers. Stir up a little drama, get people talking about whatever celebrity he was determined to shove down the public's collective throat.

I quit pacing behind my desk, seething, the anger burning a hole in me. This was a waste of time. If I were going to put an end to this, I'd have to go straight to the source. It was time for the talk that had been coming up on the horizon for much too long.

His assistant answered on the first ring. "Is he in?" I barked. Fuck wasting time on pleasantries.

"He is," she said. "Should I have him—"

"I'll be right there." The receiver slammed into the cradle while I imagined all the many creative ways to make him pay for this. Would he bother pretending he had nothing to do with it? My feet pounded the floor, but it was nothing compared to the way my heart slammed against my ribs as I stalked down the hall, passing offices where staff greeted me as I passed. I didn't have it in me to put on the happy boss act this afternoon. Not while plotting Dad's murder.

I walked in on the tail end of him popping a couple of antacids and washing them down with what looked like milk. "Swallowing all of your own lies finally started eating away at your esophagus, huh?" I asked, closing the door.

"Excuse me?" He folded his hands on the desk, looking amused. "What did I do to deserve that?"

"You had one of your photographers catch a completely innocent conversation between Danica and me yesterday," I gritted out. It was almost impossible to keep my shit together when he looked at me the way he did. Just another irritating complication. "How about that?"

"Oh, please." He waved a hand, snorting. "Grow up. If anything, it wouldn't hurt to paint you as the kind of man a woman like that wants to fuck."

What was worse? His casual crudeness or the fact he thought I needed help in that area? "I'm in a position of power over her," I reminded him. "I'm producing her next movie. You're making me look like the kind of prick who takes advantage of that if it means getting my dick wet."

"Like you've never dipped your wick into the wrong woman." He rolled his eyes, releasing a weary sigh. "This conversation is boring me and wasting my time. What is your point?"

He wanted to throw off the gloves? I could play that way too. Reaching his desk, I placed my hands on the surface and leaned in. "My point is, I've had enough of your bullshit tampering with my film and my cast. We have six weeks until the premiere. Can you handle keeping your meddling ass out of it for the next six weeks?"

There he sat, framed by the awards and photos hanging on the wall behind him. The king on his throne, wearing the sort of snide expression one expected from a monarch. I could've ripped his throat out, and not only because of today. I had more than thirty years of his bullshit under my belt.

"Are you finished?" he asked, unimpressed. "I would like to get down to business if you've finished throwing your tantrum. I've seen the rushes," he continued while I vibrated with rage. Pushing back from the desk and standing, he added, "I can't say I'm surprised that the changes I requested haven't been taken into account."

So typical. I knew this was coming. I had known for weeks. He was bound to get on my case before long once he knew I had disregarded his requests. His timing was a little transparent but unsurprising. Anything to change the subject.

"Considering we're reaching the end of principal photography..." he continued, "... that tells me you weren't planning on implementing any of them. Tell me I'm wrong. Tell me you've seen logic and reason."

"Dad, I can't see why you refuse to trust me." My body temperature jumped up close to the boiling point when he chose to laugh snidely. "Now, wait a second, dammit," I grunted out when he was about to turn away, making his eyes widen. "My entire life, you've been feeding me shit about my instincts. How good they are. How I could predict a hit by reading the script. Remember? I was eighteen years old. You brought me in as a script reader for my first internship."

"So you know a good script when you see one." He sighed. "The fact that you think the job begins and ends there tells me you're not ready for this yet."

"It was an example." I snarled. "I know damn well what makes a good movie. The difference between a hit and a flop. I know what people want to see and how they want to feel when they see it. Do you know who else does?"

Chuckling, he replied, "Let me guess. Summer Strawbridge, the next big thing. God's gift to plucky directors everywhere."

He then made a jerking-off motion with his hand that left me with no choice but to sink my short nails into my palms until I was close to breaking the skin. The man had no fucking right. He didn't know her and would never take the time to know her, to understand the first goddamn thing about her—who she was, how she thought, what made her tick.

Meeting her parents last week had taken me a long way toward understanding her. The more I knew, the more I liked her. And he had the nerve to stand there and act like a disrespectful prick because that was who he was. That was who he had always been, no matter how he pretended otherwise. The only difference between him and a man like Clyde Harris was Clyde refused to hide his true nature.

"I know what I'm doing." Staring straight into his sneering face, I growled out, "Now back off."

"I'm supposed to back off when we both know how crucial this is? I'm supposed to ignore the problems you're creating?"

"Maybe if you would get out of the way, there wouldn't be any problems," I countered. "Though I know with an ego of your size, it can take some time to get it in motion."

He surprised me by laughing, dropping into his chair again, and tilting it back. "That's right. Continue biting the hand that feeds you."

"Continue acting like you're the hand that feeds me, which we both know isn't true. Granddad's trust made sure of that." I couldn't say many good things about the old man. He was a member of the so-called old school, and rumor had it he had fallen back on the mafia more than once to fund films when times were tough at the studio. But he had put a sizable chunk of money aside for me when I was born, so much that I didn't need to rely on Dad or anyone else.

"Why do you insist on learning things the hard

way? Don't you understand?" He sighed again, rubbing his silver temples, and for the first time, I realized how old he was. It was one thing to know a number and what that number meant. It was another to see it written all over somebody's face. His jowls sagged, and the lines around his eyes were deeper than I remembered. Had he lost weight? It must've happened while he was away, those weeks he spent in Miami and New York when we first started filming. I wasn't exactly going out of my way to spend time with him and had even deliberately avoided him more than once.

"Dad... is there something you need to tell me?" We didn't exactly have anything close to a heart-to-heart. We rarely ever shared anything real, come to think of it. Our common language had always revolved around work—the studio, projections, box office numbers—that was all that mattered.

Now, I was looking at a man I hadn't bothered truly trying to see in years, maybe decades. The human being behind the name. The man sucking down Tums and milk at his desk.

What did I expect? A moment of honesty? Sincerity? A moment in which we could connect?

"I've told you everything I need to tell you," he replied, his tone short. "Now, if you wouldn't mind, I have work to do. I need to fix what you've fucked up."

"Dad, so help me," I warned, shaking. "Do not touch this movie. It's mine. You gave it to me."

"Nothing at this studio belongs to you until I say it does," he replied in an icy tone. "And considering your refusal to produce the film I told you to produce, it looks like nothing ever will be. I didn't give my life's blood to this studio all these years for you to fuck it up like some loser."

I was going to be sick. It was one thing to know the man didn't think much of me, that he kept me around for the sake of his good name, for his so-called legacy. It was another to look him in the eye while he spoke to me like I was a stranger on the street. Someone he didn't care for and never would.

I had nothing else to say. Nothing that wouldn't end with us screaming the walls down. As it was, there were voices on the other side of his door, each one representing an employee who might love nothing more than to spread gossip about the boss and his son getting into a screaming match.

"Fine," I grunted as I backed away. "Consider me gone. And if you expect me to play along and revise history so you look like the good guy in all of this, you can give it up. It's never going to happen."

"What do you think you're going to do?" he asked with a faint laugh. "What else are you cut out for?"

"According to you, I'm not even cut out to be here," I reminded him. "But don't worry. I've got more than enough resources of my own. There might come a day when you regret this. No, I'm sure there will be."

I was holding the doorknob, prepared to walk out and never come back, ready to face the consequences. "Wait," Dad barked out behind me.

So predictable. All it ever took was calling his bluff. "You mean that, don't you?" he asked. "You would walk out the door and never come back."

"That's right because I'm not going to compromise what I'm making." I turned my head, catching his eye over my shoulder. "It matters to me. To all of us, everyone who's worked on it. This is the hit we need."

"There's nothing I can say to get you to see my side of this?"

Turning slowly, I said, "That's the thing, Dad. I do see your side, but you're wrong. I know you're not used to hearing that, but you are."

He took a deep, slow breath that he released just as slowly while I watched, waiting. "Have it your way." He sighed. "I hope for everyone's sake you're right."

"You mean it?" I wasn't a child. I had given up on believing in Santa a long time ago.

"Get out of here while I'm feeling generous," he grumbled, almost growling as he gestured toward the door, swiveling his chair away from me and turning it toward the window overlooking the lot.

Could I trust him? I wasn't sure. I wanted to. I wanted to believe there wouldn't be a 'gotcha moment' where he went back on his word.

Was it really as simple as standing up to him? How many people ever had? None that I'd witnessed in all the meetings I've sat in as a kid, all the afternoons I spent doing homework in the corner while my father conducted business. He was never treated as anything less than the final word in any discussion. It was time for him to learn he was as fallible as anyone else.

It was time for me to take my place around here.

For some reason, Summer's face was the first thing that came to mind. We were in the home stretch, and soon, it wouldn't be easy to carve out the time to see her. She would be more worried than ever about optics now that those photos had gone public. I couldn't tell her Dad planted the story when explaining why he did. It would inevitably confuse and hurt her.

An idea was starting to form by the time I returned to my office. It would take calling in a lot of favors, but she was worth it. I needed one night with her, just the two of us before the already expedited process of making this movie turned into a speeding express train.

Without bothering to call Clay for confirmation beforehand, I texted Summer.

Me: *Friday. 8:00. Pack an overnight bag. No excuses.*

16

SUMMER

"Tell me I'm not making a mistake."

"You're not making a mistake." Claudia's quiet, deadpan response surprised me. I stopped halfway between the bathroom and my bedroom with a handful of toiletries waiting to be tossed into my overnight bag. She was lying on her bed with the door open, scrolling through her phone while wearing a face mask.

"Did you mean that?" I asked as I approached the doorway. "Or are you just saying it?"

"Babe." She lowered the phone to her chest, folding her hands on her stomach. "You're driving me crazy. I'm sorry. I love you, but you are."

"I'm just nervous. I don't know where he's taking

me. I don't know whether it's safe for us to even be seen together."

Groaning, she turned her head my way. "And you think he hasn't considered that?"

"That's the thing. I don't know what goes on in his head half the time." I still hadn't figured it out in the four days since he sent that cryptic, bossy text telling me to be ready at eight tonight. For once, he hadn't asked for more than I was ready to give.

The only time we'd spent together the rest of the week was in brief meetings or crossing paths at the studio. He had given me no answers about tonight.

"Maybe you shouldn't go," she suggested with a shrug. "If you think it's dangerous, you need to take care of yourself."

She had a point. *On the other hand...* "It might be fun. Lord knows I could use some before everything gets nuts in these final weeks."

Just the thought made me feel shaky and uneasy. It was almost time for the world to judge my work. It was one thing for me to know everybody at Cannes had watched our movie, but my name wasn't on it. If they had hated it, I could've sat back and pretended to have nothing to do with it. It wouldn't be my reputation on the line.

This time, there was no such luck. I had to

believe they'd love it, and not only because I had put so much of myself into it, but because if it didn't work out, I would also be really and truly screwed.

"Do what you think is right," Claudia concluded, returning to her phone. "If you don't mind, I'm engaging in a little self-care because my boss has been running me ragged."

"Your boss loves you," I reminded her.

"Which is why I'm still here," she fired back, and it looked like she was almost smiling under her sheet mask.

In the end, I was ready for Lex's driver at exactly eight. This time, instead of picking me up at a seedy motel, he carried my bag through the courtyard of the apartment complex, where a handful of my temporary neighbors stopped and watched. Maybe they were wondering who I was and why I was so important. The idea had me biting back a smile by the time we reached the sidewalk, and he opened the back door for me.

"What is your name?" I asked as I slid in.

"Carl," he replied, closing the door and looking surprised I would ask.

"Thank you, Carl." I always told myself if I were ever in a situation like this, I would acknowledge and thank the people helping me by their first name to make sure they knew they were seen and appreciated.

Once he was in the driver's seat, I asked, "I guess you wouldn't be able to tell me where we're going, huh?"

"Mr. Landry only gave me the address. I'm sure if he didn't tell you, he wants it to remain a surprise."

I settled in and tried my best not to let nerves get the better of me. It would be fine. He knew what he was doing and wouldn't take risks. Still, this was the first time we'd be anywhere that didn't involve the studio or his house. Where could we go where nobody would know we were there?

My question was sort of answered as Carl pulled into the parking garage underneath what looked like a hotel high-rise. An empty garage, I realized, as we rolled through. It was sort of eerie, the rows and rows of empty spaces. Why were we here?

He pulled to a stop in front of a pair of elevator doors and got out to open my door. "Is this place closed?" I whispered, and even that echoed in the empty concrete space.

"Mr. Landry asked me to give you this." He handed me an envelope, grinning. "And to wait until you get on the elevator. Then, I'm allowed to leave."

"This is all very confusing," I admitted as I

opened the envelope, pulling out the note card inside. A brief message was scrawled on it.

Press P.

"That's it?" I stared down at the handwriting. "P? I don't get it."

"Maybe P for Penthouse?" He nodded toward the elevator. "Go ahead."

Well, the poor guy probably wanted to go home. I had to trust Lex wasn't leading me into some weird, twisted game as I stepped onto the elevator. Sure enough, there was a button marked P. With my overnight bag in one hand, I pressed the button, then waved to Carl as the doors slid shut with a soft whoosh.

This was crazy. I was riding an elevator in what looked like an abandoned building, all because Lex told me to. The absurdity made me laugh, which was a small miracle considering how nervous I was. It helped ease some of the tension, so I felt more comfortable by the time the doors opened onto a spacious suite.

The top floor was definitely not abandoned the way the empty garage made it look. It was stunning, warmly lit, and lavishly furnished, with windows directly across from where I stood overlooking downtown Los Angeles. The Hollywood sign glowed in the distance like a beacon, drawing me closer and pulling me through the living room until I stood in front of the glass.

"Hello."

I spun on my heel, gasping in surprise. I was too busy drooling over the view to hear Lex come in. The sight of him in a white linen suit took my breath away. It made his tanned skin gleam, while the open buttons at the top of his blue shirt hinted at the broad chest underneath. I was glad I had gone all out on a new black dress, silver sandals, and the lacy thong I was wearing underneath.

"Okay, this is beautiful," I admitted. "But what is it? I would have guessed it was abandoned from the looks of it."

"When you're involved in a project, that's all you pay attention to." He wasn't chiding me. It wasn't criticism. He was chuckling as he approached, holding out a hand to take my bag. "Let me show you around."

"But *where* are we?"

He took my hand and led the way. "My good friend, Clayton Manning, is around a month from opening this hotel to the public. It's been in the news lately. They're going to have a huge party to celebrate the grand opening."

"So no one else is staying here right now? We have the entire hotel to ourselves?"

"That's right. It's us and the security team I hired for the night." When I gasped, he shrugged. "Just in case. I want to be sure you're safe."

It was hard to believe. Not only was he ridiculously wealthy, but he had friends who could set him up like this. He also had the ability to hire a security team for the night. "It's amazing," I concluded as he continued leading me through the enormous suite.

"You haven't seen the best part." It was no surprise when we ended up in the bedroom, where there were views just as stunning as the ones I admired in the living room. He left my bag on the floor at the foot of the king-size bed, then continued leading me to a door in the far corner of the room.

"You're going to show me the closet?" I asked, arching a brow.

"Not exactly." He opened it to reveal a staircase leading up. There was a second door at the top, and when he opened it, I could barely breathe from the anticipation leading here.

"What do you think?" he asked. "It's all ours for the night."

I let go of his hand in a slow circle to admire everything. A sparkling pool right there on the roof.

A canopy draped over the top of it, the underside strung from end to end with twinkling lights. The night was beautiful, clear and warm, and a gentle breeze created ripples on the water that sent light dancing everywhere. Lit torches added to the ambiance, along with soft music piped in through some invisible source. It was magical.

"I called in a favor, and Clay had the pool filled and prepared for us. I ordered dinner, too," Lex added, gesturing toward a candlelit table surrounded by potted palms and lush, fragrant tropical flowers.

It was like stepping into a garden in a world of our own. Nobody could see us. We were on top of the world. I walked over to the waist-high wall edging the roof on all sides, standing on tiptoe to look over the edge and down at the traffic below.

"Like it?" His soft question tore my attention away from the twinkling lights stretching out below us. The light playing off the pool's ripples washed over his face and made his dark eyes glow. Or maybe that was a trick of my mind, buzzing, excited, and overwhelmed.

My heart swelled as I said, "I love it. I can't believe you went to all this trouble to make sure we were safe."

He stepped up behind me, and I smiled when his lips found my neck. "You smell fantastic," he whispered, growling softly before burying his nose in my hair.

"Isn't this beautiful?" I asked, overwhelmed, leaning against him while the breeze rustled my hair and his hands slid over my hips.

"I was going to say the same thing, but not about the view." His arms wound around my waist, and one hand slid up over my stomach, finally cupping my breast. "You could rule this town. You know that?"

"You're just saying that," I whispered, caught between the sizzling sensations his touch brought about and the breathtaking future he was creating in my imagination. It was one thing for me to believe I could make it, but for him to say it?

"Why would I say that if it wasn't true? What, you think I'm trying to seduce you?" His thumb brushed my nipple and made it tighten before he moved back down to my hips. "I think we both know that's not necessary at this point."

"It's what I want... more than anything." I stared at the sign in the distance. There was a premiere going on downtown, and crisscrossing beams of light flashed and danced across the sky. It could be me down there, having my picture taken, waving to fans.

His kisses were slower now, more sensual, his breath deeper. The fire he always lit in me burned bright already, hotter with every caress, every touch of his lips. "You have what it takes to be one of the greats. You have the instincts, and you're sure as hell stubborn enough."

My laughter ended on a gasp when his hands slid up under my dress and stroked my thighs. The pressure of his erection against my ass was impossible to ignore, and instinct made me push back and grind against it. There was nothing like the sound of his needy, breathless groans. Power surged in me when I heard it, knowing I drove him to that. I could make him lose his grip on himself.

"Imagine it." He probed between my thighs, so I parted them to give him room. The first touch against my moist lips was electric and mind-blowing. I didn't know if it was the excitement of being with him or imagining myself down there running the town, making it mine. Either way, my slit was a river he eagerly dipped into, sliding his fingers through my wetness before easing them deep inside me.

"Imagine having everything you want," he

murmured, breathing hard while his fingers moved in and out. I reached behind me and found his bulge, rubbing it in time with his strokes. "Calling the shots. Signing your own checks. Choosing your projects, your dream casts." I squeezed him gently, and his teeth grazed my earlobe. "Fuck, you're so hot. I want to fuck you so badly," he growled out, making me shiver. "All day, no matter where I am, I'd always rather be like this, with you."

I had to be dreaming. But no, this was very real—the sound and smell of him, the pressure of his thick digits working me into a frenzy.

"I want you here," he rasped. "I need you. I'm going to fuck you out here in the open where no one can see."

That was the best idea I'd heard all night. He reached into his pocket, and I lowered my thong to my knees, bending over a little. He had turned me into a brazen hussy, and I loved every second of it, especially now with the hint of danger and wickedness.

The opening of the foil packet was quickly followed by familiar pressure against my pussy. I held my breath, waiting, then moaned out my approval when he sank himself deep. "Fuck, so wet," he said through gritted teeth, taking me by the hips and holding me in place. He leaned down, breathing in my ear. "So wet for me. Look at you. Getting fucked forty stories above Beverly Hills. You love it, don't you? You wouldn't be so wet if you didn't."

"Y-yesss," I moaned out, turning my head to find his mouth. His tongue touched mine, playful, teasing, stroking in time with his impossibly thick cock. I couldn't take it. It was all too much. Too good.

"And are you gonna come for me while all those people are down there?" he asked, covering my mouth, plunging his tongue inside, making it so I could only moan my response.

I was going to come, and it was going to be massive. The tension built, tightening my muscles, tightening me around him.

"Shit... you're gonna make me come..." he whispered, moving faster, harder, our bodies slapping together until there was nothing for me to do but howl, lost in release, lost in sensation, lost in him. I was lost in everything about him and the world he was showing me—a world I wanted so much to be part of.

I shouted it all out, my head tilted back, my eyes open to stare up at the night sky. By the time he finished and pulled out, I was weak, spent. Happy. Genuinely happy.

What if this was it? What if we could be something together? Because I wasn't sure I would be able to give him up when this was all over.

"I'd suggest we take a swim to cool off now," he murmured, kissing my cheek and stepping back. "But I'm fucking starving. How about we test the food?"

Like I would've said no to anything he suggested at a moment like that. "We have all night, right?" I reminded him with a grin.

17

LEX

It was easy to understand why Dad used to get so frazzled and distant when one of his films was coming close to the finish line.

If it weren't for my phone being on me at all times, I would forget what day it was. I'd sat in more meetings over the past two weeks than I ever remember sitting through in all the years since I started working with the company. To think, I got bored out of my mind going through budget meetings and such—the shit work Dad used to assign me.

At these meetings, people looked at me for answers, confirmation, or the go-ahead to keep moving in one direction or another. When I wasn't sitting in conference rooms or on Zoom, I was crunching numbers, researching tactics to get this movie in front of as many people as possible. 'Good enough' wouldn't be enough this time around. We had to crush all expectations. Dad's methods might have worked back in the old days, but in a world of digital distractions, what mattered was rising above the noise.

"If the studio were mine, my first act would be to replace all the older staff in the promotions department." I pulled off my tie and tossed it onto an armchair just inside my bedroom door. It was past ten o'clock, and I had just gotten home after a stuffy business dinner. There had been countless nights in the past when I hadn't gotten home until nearly dawn, and I never felt this exhausted. Was I turning into an old man before my time?

"Wow," Summer murmured on the other end of the call. "That sounds terrible. What's the age cut-off going to be? Forty? Fifty? What are you going to do to the people then? Drive them out to a farm where they can play with all the other people you put out to pasture for being too old?"

Now that she put it that way, my idea soured. "I'm not saying I would fire them, only that I might reassign them somewhere in the company. Same pay, if not more. It's not even a matter of age," I concluded, dropping to the bed to take off my shoes.

"What is it, then?" She was back at her apartment after a long day of her own. That was all we had in front of us from now until the premiere in four weeks. Long days. Connecting over the phone was the safest way to spend time with her lately.

"The ability to be flexible," I replied as I started unbuttoning my shirt. "A guy may be seventy years old, and it wouldn't matter so long as he was willing to keep up with current practices. I don't care what worked back in the eighties or nineties. That was a different world."

"I guess it's not easy for people to let go of what has worked for them for so long. I mean, look at your dad."

Like I needed her to remind me of him. My teeth ground together at the thought. "That's not the same. He thinks he knows everything, anyway. It wouldn't matter how old he was."

"I know, but he's coming around. He likes what we did with the movie, and let's face it. Landry International hasn't put out anything like this in a long, long time. Something with action and a plot, you know? He's adjusting."

I would let her hold onto her illusions. There was no use correcting her just so I could say I was right. "I know. That's true."

"Can I ask you something?" I heard the water running on her end. It was nice to imagine her puttering around, making herself tea or whatever it was she was doing. A distraction from the responsibilities of the day. "Before, you said if you ever owned the studio... something close to that, anyway. What do you mean if? I thought that was the assumed outcome."

I froze halfway through, pulling the shirt from my waistband. "Did I say it that way?"

"You did. How come?"

"Freudian slip?" When she didn't laugh, I gave up the act. "To be honest with you, I've never seen myself in his position."

"You're kidding! Why did you never say that?"

"It never came up," I pointed out. "And it isn't the end of the world."

"What would you do otherwise?" She made it sound like the most unbelievable concept ever. "Well, I guess you wouldn't need to work, really..."

It was a relief to be free of what had felt like a straitjacket all day. I left the shirt and pants to be picked up for dry cleaning before sliding into a pair of soft shorts. "I would still be here, at the studio. But I'm more interested in *making* movies. Not sitting behind a desk, trying to figure out how to squeeze another dime out of the budget. I'd want to be the person behind the camera if possible."

I had never admitted that to another living soul. Not even Spencer, my oldest friend. It was almost like ripping open a wound. A vulnerable feeling. What did I expect? For her to make fun of me?

"I had no idea you felt that way."

I couldn't tell what she thought. She was working hard to hide her reaction. "What, you don't think I can't do it?" I asked.

"Jesus Christ! Why would you jump to that conclusion?" Her laughter echoed in what sounded like the kitchen. "I just didn't know you would ever want to direct. What kind of movies? Do you have any projects in mind?"

"Down, girl." It was a relief to know she didn't think less of me opening up, yes, but her excitement was a little overwhelming.

Her frustrated little grunt wasn't surprising. "Don't tell me you haven't thought about it. I bet you see scripts all the time that you would love to make."

"Now that you mention it..."

"I knew it!" she crowed, laughing. "What is it? Tell me about it."

"It was a Cold War thriller. This was years ago," I explained as I walked barefoot from my dressing room to the bedroom. I could almost imagine her here with me, the two of us connecting after a busy day. "I was only interning at the time. Reading scripts, providing synopses. It fucking crackled, I swear to God. I couldn't stop flipping through the pages. I saw the whole thing in my head, exactly how I would want it shot."

"So what happened?"

"It got stuck in development hell for a few years, and the last I heard, it was shelved permanently."

I heard a spoon clinking against a cup, like she was stirring her drink. "It makes me sad, thinking about how many potentially classic movies are shelved like that before anybody ever gets the chance to turn them into something real."

"I feel the same way." She had no idea how many scripts got rejected every day. Not marketable, too cerebral, too expensive, the list went on.

Her enthusiasm was endless, it seemed. "But that's the kind of movie you're interested in?" she asked. "Thrillers, that kind of thing?"

"I think so. A little drama, a little excitement. I've always been drawn to them."

"If you could remake any movie, which one would it be?"

"Oh, you can't do that!" I pulled my blankets up, then flipped off the light next to the bed. It was a little early for me. At least, it was early when my life wasn't completely upside down. I had a seven-thirty breakfast meeting, though, then another at nine halfway across town. I had to be sharp.

"Says who?" she teased. "I'll tell you mine if you tell me yours."

"It's not just one movie," I decided. It was almost like settling into bed with her, having her voice in my ear. "There's so many. It's to the point where I have a hard time enjoying a movie because all I can think about is what I would do differently."

"Oh my God," she whispered. "I know what you mean. It's like, I can't take any pleasure from watching movies anymore. All I can ever do is think about how I would have framed a scene or if I would've held a shot a few seconds longer."

"Yes!" She got it. I should've known she would.

"You know what I need to know now, right?" There was something wicked in her giggle. "You know what's coming. You have to."

I hadn't until she brought it up. "No," I told her. "I never imagined what I would shoot differently with this movie. That's the truth."

"Good answer." We laughed together again, more softly this time. I imagined her sipping herbal tea, curled up in her bed where we spent that first night together months ago. It felt like half a lifetime had passed since then.

"So what are you wearing?" I asked because I had to. There was no way I could be in bed, speaking to her, and not think about what we should be doing together.

"Do you want the honest answer?" she asked. "Or the answer you're looking for?"

"Let's go with option B."

"Oh, Mr. Landry." The formality of my name slipping off her tongue shouldn't have stirred my cock, but it did. Suddenly, her voice went breathy and high-pitched like a bad Marilyn Monroe imper-sonation. "I'm wearing this itty-bitty little night-gown. It's see-through. You can see my nipples straight through it, and I'm not wearing any underwear."

It was supposed to be a joke. What a shame my dick didn't have a sense of humor. "What color is it?" I asked.

"Pale pink," she whispered. "Just as pink as... I can't say."

"You can." I was getting harder by the second. I pictured her like that, wearing a scrap of see-through fabric. "Just as pink as your pussy? Is that what you were going to say?"

"Yes," she purred. "Now, do you want to hear what I'm really wearing?"

"No, let's talk more about that nightgown." I reached into my shorts, and my dick jumped at the brush of my fingers. I would've much rather had her touching me, caressing, wrapping her tapered fingers around my aching shaft.

"Are you touching yourself right now?" she asked. "I can hear the way you're breathing. The way it's getting faster."

"I'm holding onto my cock right now, baby." It twitched and jumped in my hand as I closed my eyes and settled back, focusing on the mental image of Summer on her hands and knees, crawling up the bed, the sheer nightgown she described sliding over her skin.

"Is it me you're thinking about?" she whispered.

The fucking tease.

"Just you." Precum dribbled from my tip, and I swiped a thumb across it, using it to lube me, moving faster. "What about you? Are you touching your pussy now, thinking about me?"

"Yes..." she moaned, "... oh God, yes. I'm playing with my clit like it's your tongue licking me."

Fuck. Images of her legs spread wide, giving me a look at those glistening, pink folds passed in a blur, and I could almost taste her as I fucked my fist, listening as her soft whimpers got quicker, more urgent.

"Shi-it, Lex, yes..." she panted, "... mmm, yeah, that's good... faster... just like that..."

My fist was a blur, tightening the way her pussy would. "Would you like that? My tongue slipping through your folds, flicking your clit... " I whispered, groaning when she did. My balls lifted in time with her high-pitched whine, and I let go, coming until my ears rang while she whimpered and moaned.

"Oh God." She sighed, still breathless. "That was not where I saw this conversation going."

"You should know by now there's always a chance of the conversation going that way when it's me you're talking to..." I paused to catch my breath, listening as she caught hers. "So, what were you really wearing?"

"No, let's not destroy the fantasy," she decided. A fantasy. That was all this was, really. When I looked at the other pillow on my bed, it was empty. Her head wasn't on it. It wouldn't be until the movie premiered. She wanted to play it cool after that brief flare-up with Danica, and I understood why.

She was right too. There was always someone watching, waiting for somebody to fuck up so they could profit from it. I could withstand that kind of a mistake, but she couldn't.

18

SUMMER

This was it. This was what it had all boiled down to. The endless hours, the nights spent sleeping on the tiny sofa in my office—when I slept at all, which wasn't always guaranteed.

An enormous bouquet of white roses arranged in a crystal vase waited on my desk when I reached my office the morning we were scheduled to screen my movie in full for the first time. My heart skipped a beat before I crossed the room and found the card tucked among the blooms.

Knock them dead today. - L

The nerves I had wrestled with all morning and most of last night eased a little. My chest loosened. I could breathe... sort of.

Alexander Landry would be there, along with the film's principal investors and other studio executives. The idea made cold sweat bead on the back of my neck, but I shook it off, determined not to let it get to me. They had to love it. I hadn't spent days on end sitting with the editors, tweaking every last detail and polishing it until it shone for this to flop. I had never been so sure of anything as I was of this movie.

My only hope was they felt the same way. The thing about art was its subjectiveness. The viewer always brought with them their own perceptions and expectations.

Please let them put all of that aside for today.

Claudia was in bed with a nasty summer cold, and I had promised to call her as soon as it was over. *"You've got this,"* she'd reminded me as I left the apartment this morning. *"Knock 'em dead."*

I planned to.

Everything I knew to be true ran through my head all at once as I crossed the lot on my way to the screening room. I knew what I was doing. I was damn good at it. I had Lex to back me up all the way. We had worked hard, doing great things.

And this was just the first of many victories. Like he said while he was inside me on that hotel roof—I was going to own this town. I was never so sure of it as when I stepped into the room where numerous men in suits waited.

One of them was Lex, who offered a secretive little smile when our eyes met. My body ached for him—his arms around me, most of all. I needed his strength and confidence when mine was in short supply.

"And there she is." Alexander stood and extended a hand, cordial as ever. "I've been looking forward to today," he informed me with one of his million-dollar megawatt smiles. It was easy to see where his son got his charm because the man practically oozed it.

"So have I," I told him. There was a seat open in the front row, center, which I guessed they were saving for me. I would much rather have sat in the back, watching their reactions, but maybe this was better. If they cringed, flinched, or gave each other funny looks, I wouldn't have to see it.

Lex gave me a tiny nod, taking his seat at the end of my row, three seats down. "Let's begin," he announced loudly enough for the guy in the booth to hear him.

It was like going up the first hill on a roller coaster. I gripped the armrests with both hands, my heart in my throat, my breath coming in short bursts until my yoga training kicked in, and I consciously forced myself to breathe slowly.

It would've been better if I'd let myself hyperventilate and pass out.

All it took was five minutes, maybe less, for dread to take root in my gut. My breathing, once so erratic, turned tight and shallow, almost scorching my lungs. But nothing hurt worse than the fiery coal lodged in my chestnothing burned worse than the burning coal lodged in my chest.

This wasn't my movie. Not the way I made it.

I glanced over at Lex, hoping against hope this was a joke. Some sort of prank, a *welcome to the studio* kind of thing. I was still that desperate for none of this to be real. He stared at the screen, brows drawn together, his lips slightly parted. Confused?

Absolutely. I know I was utterly baffled. I wanted to leave, yet I felt compelled to stay, to watch what unfolded before me and try to make sense of it all. Minutes passed, endless minutes where I had no choice but to watch a parade of scenes someone cobbled together. They were scenes I had shot, but they were out of order. There were bits and pieces cut out that ruined the context. Around thirty minutes in, there was a montage featuring various cuts of Danica and the supporting actresses washing cars. They had played around a little, spraying each other with the hoses, and I had let it go because I figured they were having a good time, and happy actresses led to better work. Some fucking genius decided to turn it into an actual scene, and they no doubt planned on layering pulse-pounding music on top once the score was added.

After an hour, I checked out. It was safer that way for everyone involved. My nails dug into my palms long enough that I hardly felt the pain after a while. It was nothing compared to the pain in my heart, anyway. How did this happen? Why? Wasn't my work good enough as it was? Why couldn't they leave it alone?

Had they ever planned on releasing the movie I filmed? Or were they always going to do this?

And did he know? How much did he have to do with it?

When it was over, I couldn't move. I couldn't pull my gaze away from the blank screen now that the last of the movie was finished rolling. There were a few seconds of silence so profound that I could've heard a pin drop if it wasn't for the pounding in my ears.

It was Alexander who spoke first, in a loud voice

that filled the room. "It looks like we have a block-buster on our hands, people."

I had to be imagining this. This was all a sick, twisted dream where a bunch of people erupted in applause over a piece of shit that the world would forget in a week, if that. It might not even take that long for them to dismiss it and move on to the next thing because the public, in general, didn't have a long memory.

It would be forgotten, pushed over to streaming within a month of the premiere. And then it would be time for The Next Big Thing, while I had a piece of shit under my belt that wouldn't get me a job anywhere. Not a job I wanted, at least.

"Bravo!" one of the men called out, which led to a round of applause that was somehow worse than anything so far.

No. There was something even worse than that. The way Lex sat there, staring at me, his eyes wide and seemingly sunken into a pale face. This was his chance to stand up and ask what the hell this was all about. What happened to our movie? Who did this? How could we undo it?

He could have...

... but he didn't.

"Now is as good a time as any to make an announcement." Alexander worked his way to the end of his row, then walked down the short series of stairs until he reached the bottom row and came to a stop beside a frozen Lex. "The premiere of this film will mark the beginning of a new era for Landy International. I intend to step aside and name Lex as my successor."

Lex reeled like somebody hit him, but his father pulled him to his feet and wrapped him in a bear hug. That was what it was all about. Making the movie his daddy really wanted to prove he could handle the studio.

I couldn't sit there another minute, listening to the applause, the smug self-congratulation as they all patted each other on the back and projected box office numbers. Was I supposed to sit here and pretend there was nothing wrong? Of course, because that's all that mattered. Pretending. And I thought I wanted to be part of this?

"Summer?" Alexander called out by the time I was halfway out the door. I didn't trust myself to respond or even act like I heard him. I settled for fleeing flat-out, rushing down the hall and out the door into the brilliant, sunshiny day. How was the world turning? How were people going about their business like it was any ordinary morning? Didn't they know the world was ending?

"Summer!" I heard Lex behind me but didn't acknowledge him. I needed to get away. To get my shit from the office and get the hell out of this godforsaken town. It had only ever broken my heart. I could honestly say my parents were right all along. I had no hope of surviving around here.

"Goddammit, Summer. Wait! Please!" Lex didn't catch up with me until I was already in my office, where that arrangement of flowers only taunted me now. Fuck finding my peaceful center. I picked it up and threw it to the floor in time for him to witness my rage.

"You motherfucker!" I snarled as broken crystal scattered across the floor in all directions. "How could you? Why did you do this?"

"I didn't do anything!" He had the nerve to stand there, looking shocked and innocent, like he was the wounded party. It was like it was his work that had been so callously disregarded, and he was the one someone had lied to. Like somebody had asked him to sit back and pretend everything was okay when it definitely wasn't. What, was I supposed to never say a word about my movie being butchered to hell?

"I cannot believe you. No, actually," I decided. "I

can absolutely believe you. I can't believe myself for being so fucking stupid!" It was all so ugly and painful and sad. The whole thing was so sad. I could've cried myself to death over it.

With his hands held in front of him, he urged, "You have to let me explain."

"I don't have to do a damn thing," I reminded him. How was I so blind? I couldn't really blame him. He was only behaving as his nature made him. I was the one who walked willingly into the trap. Forcing myself to forget everything I knew, and for what? A big dick? I had betrayed myself, and now there was a ruined movie to show for it.

"I didn't do that." When I laughed at his lies, he grunted out, "Summer, I swear, I didn't!"

"So it was magic? The movie I made, a movie with heart and soul and intelligence, mysteriously turned into a brainless, testosterone-fueled mess? You expect me to believe that? How gullible do you think I am? No, don't answer that," I added, almost spitting the words. "I know exactly how stupid you think I am."

He blew out a trembling breath and was quieter when he spoke again. "Please, let me explain. I know, I should've told you—"

"So you admit this has your fingerprints all over it!"

"No, dammit, that's not what I mean. Yes," he barked out. "I knew the sort of movie Dad wanted. The studio needs a win. But all these months, I've bent over backward trying to convince him the movie you made is that win." When I didn't react right away, he asked, "Why don't we sit down?" He even had the nerve to gesture toward the sofa, like I was going to be so easily placated into having a sit-down talk where he would undoubtedly feed me more lies.

And damn him, I wanted to believe them, which was why I couldn't give him the chance. "I have nothing to say to you," I whispered, shaking my head and backing away when he reached for me.

His arms dropped to his sides. "I've been behind you from the beginning."

"There's a joke." I snarled. "From the beginning, you told me who my cast would be. What my timeline was. I'm supposed to believe you didn't go in and edit my film until it's practically Swiss cheese? I lost count of all the plot holes now that scenes were taken out and moved around! It doesn't make any goddamn sense!" It came out as a cry straight from my heart, and I wasn't only talking about the movie. Nothing made sense anymore.

When all he did was stand there with his mouth hanging open, bitter tears welled in my eyes. He had no defense because there was none. He knew what he had done. He knew what it meant. Between hitching, silent sobs, I whispered, "I will never forgive you for this."

He pushed up his sleeves, grunting as he did. Glaring at me now that he knew his lies wouldn't get him anywhere. "I've been fighting for this movie from the beginning. I refused to give my father what he wanted. I only wanted the movie you wanted to make, Summer. I don't give a shit whether or not you believe me. It's the truth, and I know it. I guess that will have to be enough."

"Oh, you fucking hero." I smirked, giving him a slow clap. "And when they make a movie of your life, who do you think will play you? I mean, a story like this should be shared with the world. Make sure they include the gripping climax where you climb over my carcass to claim your place at the head of the studio."

"Sure. Take it out on me." He sneered. "The only goddamn person who's been on your side through all of this."

"Newsflash, genius! You have not been on my side because you allowed that to happen! I don't care if you did it yourself or not, it happened under your nose. You're supposed to be fighting for us!"

Before he could plead with me and insist he had, I held up my hands in surrender. "You know what? Save yourself the trouble. I don't want you to fight for me, and I don't need you to. I forgot I've never been able to depend on anybody but myself. But thank you for the reminder," I concluded. "Get the hell out of my sight."

"You think it's that easy?" he demanded as his face darkened along with his eyes. "You think I'm going to just let you walk away?"

"You don't have a choice." I was almost sorry for him. He was that deluded, that sure of his power over me.

My reaction made him growl before he muttered, "Remember, you're contracted. The press junket. The premiere."

Dear God. I was so busy falling apart that I forgot all about that. The idea of sitting around and pretending to be proud of the piece of shit I was just forced to watch made my stomach turn. "No way. I'm not doing it."

"It's nice that you think you have a choice, but

you don't." He shrugged, folding his arms. At the end of the day, it was always going to boil down to the studio and his image and money.

"Sue me. What the hell do I care? No, you know what?" I asked when a better idea came to mind. "Aside from what I've spent already and the money I used to pay Claudia, you can have the rest back. The entire balance of my fee for this film. I'll pay the rest back if I have to. That's how determined I am to have nothing to do with any of this."

"You would do that? You would shoot yourself in the foot just to prove a point?" Before I could answer, he shook his head. "What the hell am I saying? Of course, you would. This is who you've always been. Listen to me." He surprised me by approaching, the urgency in his voice written on his face. I backed away again, bringing him to a halt before he sighed. "What I saw back there? It makes me sick to see what they did. But I am not giving you permission to walk away. You don't get to wash your hands of this."

"What are you, my father? Don't tell me what you will or won't give me permission to do!" Could people hear us outside? Did I care? Hell, I hoped they did. All those people walking around, kissing his ass, treating him like the second coming. They deserved to know what a spineless, cowardly piece of shit he actually was.

His shoulders heaved. His hands tightened into fists. "You know it won't be that easy. Though the way you're acting, it might be better if you don't participate in the press junket." Still, his eyes narrowed in a steely glare. "But you will show up at the premiere, and you will play nice. The rest of it, we can brush under the rug."

"Yes, I'm sure you're very good at that."

"Don't do this," he whispered, like a last-ditch effort. "Don't push me away. We need each other now. We can find a way out of this."

Wouldn't that be nice? To fall into his arms and believe whatever he said. To betray myself again. "You can take your false promises and shove them up your ass," I whispered back.

"But..." he blew out a deep breath, trembling, "... I love you." His voice was soft, desperate, vulnerable, and it almost was my undoing. ~~I'd die here and now.~~ There was no way I could survive. Not once I heard those words come out of his mouth.

I love you too. My heart screamed it loud enough that I was surprised he couldn't hear. "Another lie," I whispered, making him cringe. "Love?" I snorted out, throwing my hands up as if the universe had just cracked a cosmic joke. "Well, that's another lie. The only person you love is your goddamn self!"

My bag was on my chair. I grabbed it, as it was the only thing in the room that was really mine. My laptop and everything else were at the apartment. "As for me, I'm going home where I belong. See you at the premiere, Mr. Landry."

His face fell. "Wait—"

"I swear to God," I said. "I will kill you if I have to look at you a second longer. I cannot stomach the sight of you." He made the mistake of getting in my way, and I shoved as hard as I could. Somehow, the mixture of my rage and his surprise was enough to make him stumble backward. I marched past him and out the door, searching desperately for my phone with a hand that shook so badly I could barely get a hold of it.

But I did, and I called Claudia. She picked up as I slid behind the wheel of my car. "How did it go?" she asked, chipper in spite of her stuffy nose.

That was all it took. Her hopeful, eager greeting. That was all I needed for my resolve to break along with my heart. Covering my face with one hand, I sobbed. "We're leaving. I'm packing everything, and we're leaving as soon as possible. It's over. It's all over."

It had never really begun.

19

—————

LEX

Shattered crystal glittered on the floor, sparkling around the discarded roses. Something that had been so beautiful was now destroyed. What a perfect symbol.

I was in shock. Somehow, I couldn't wrap my mind around what just happened. The movie was cut and pasted and reconfigured until it was more like Frankenstein's monster than anything Summer had originally filmed. My father's audacity at pretending there was nothing out of the ordinary about the whole situation. His ass-kissing sycophants applauding like they just watched fucking *Citizen Kane* or some shit.

And his announcement that he was stepping aside, handing over the reins.

I could hardly pin down any one of my confused, angry, disappointed thoughts. We had lost something good, and not only in terms of the footage Summer shot.

This wasn't the time to think about her. I'd end up shutting down completely since the thought of her walking out of my life forever was too much to comprehend. No, I had one thing and one thing only that required immediate attention. I couldn't let myself lapse into personal shit when there was betrayal to deal with. That meant slowly walking out of the office, where I left the shattered ruins of Summer's bouquet, then turned down the hall, walking straight to Dad's office.

The voices around me blended into noise that did nothing to permeate the shock still gripping me.

How could he?

How could I?

I'd sat there without saying a word, stunned at first, then self-preserving. We were in mixed company at the time, and I was seriously considering murder. No wonder she felt betrayed.

How was I supposed to make this up to her? Something she had looked forward to long before stepping foot through the studio gates. Her first major film, a dream come true. From where she stood, that dream had been thrown in her face.

I strode past his assistant's desk and into the empty room. He wasn't back yet, probably still patting himself on the back. I sat behind his desk, something that wasn't lost on me, symbolism-wise. This would be officially mine.

I had never wanted it less.

He didn't keep me waiting long. For all I knew, he got a call telling him there was a loud fight. My pulse pounded a little harder with every footstep, louder until he sauntered into the room wearing a patented Alexander Landry shit-eating grin. "What did I tell you? Your old man still knows a thing or two about what's going to work."

His smug attitude made me sick, though battling the urge to puke was easier than fighting the desire to hurt him. "You honestly believe that, don't you?" I asked. "Somehow, you have deluded yourself into believing whatever it was I just watched is something worth being proud of."

Laughing indulgently, he pointed to the desk. "That's not yours quite yet. And you're welcome, by the way," he added as he approached while I stood. "Silly me, expecting thanks."

"We both know you timed that announcement

carefully." He had played me like a fiddle from the beginning. I was clueless or arrogant enough to believe him. "To keep me from ripping your goddamn head off."

He lowered himself into his chair with a sigh. "Son, that is exactly where you're wrong about this whole thing. It's better for you to learn it now. Pride is a useless goal to strive for. It doesn't last. And it doesn't satisfy investors. You want to be proud? Be proud of all the money your movie is going to make."

When I scoffed, his brows lifted. "It means there will still be a studio for you to run. Did it ever occur to you that I did this for you? Knowing I would step back, handing you something that will survive?"

"But the movie is garbage. You have to know it."

"It's a hit," he fired back, waving a hand. "You think people want to go to the movies to think? To learn how challenging it is for a woman to make it in racing? Give me a fucking break! They want to be entertained. They want to see a little skin. They want to be excited. They want to forget the shit going on outside that theater. That is what we're providing."

"Well, good luck with it." I waved a hand, prepared to leave the room and the studio. I'd had more than enough. "I wasn't bluffing when I said I would leave, so your fake offer to retire was wasted."

"I *am* retiring," he insisted as I walked away. "At the suggestion of my oncologist."

I had to give it to him. He always had a talent for pulling the rug from under me. I froze, the word reverberating through me. *Oncologist.*

Turning slowly, I searched his face, his body language for some sign he was screwing with my head. I found nothing but a weary old man. "Dad," I choked out. "You have cancer?"

"I've got this thing in my stomach," he grumbled. "They found it early and the doc has hope it'll pass with surgery and radiation. But I need to rest, and I think we both know that's not possible around here."

As I sputtered, fighting to make sense of it all, he asked, "Do you understand now? Throwing your attitude at me, calling me everything under the sun when I'm trying to leave you with something here. That's all I ever wanted to do. I couldn't hand over the reins, knowing there won't be anything left to give you."

There was a hollow feeling in my chest as I approached, finally sitting on the corner of his desk. "Why didn't you tell me before now?"

"I didn't want to see the look you have on your face right now, for one thing," he grumbled. "I'm going to be fine. I'll step back, spending the rest of my life enjoying the fruits of my labor. Let's not start casting my biopic just yet."

His choice of words brought to mind one of Summer's many scathing comments and hardened my attitude a little. He was sick. He had his reasons, but he was still wrong. "You had no right to do what you did to her. You had to know it would kill her."

"She'll get over it."

"I don't think so," I murmured with a sinking heart. It was easy for him to say. To him, she was a means to an end. His diversity hire. Slap her name on the project, earn some brownie points, make a mint. She wasn't real to him.

"Oh no." I looked his way in time to see his eyes roll. "You didn't. Tell me you didn't fuck the girl."

"Charming," I muttered. "The point is, she's a human being. You used her and had the balls to act like there was nothing out of the ordinary about what happened earlier. Like she should've been grateful and kept her mouth shut."

"Which is exactly what she should've done."

"You're wrong." Standing, I shook my head. "I'm

going to make things right. You want to hand over the studio? Fine. Which means I'm calling the shots now."

He sat up straighter. "Wait—"

"You made the announcement. I'll have a press release written up to confirm it." With one last glare, I added, "Try me."

"Do you know what I went through to get that film edited behind her back?" he demanded, almost jumping from his chair. For a sick man, he had plenty of energy.

"I don't care. You wasted your time." With a shrug, I backed away. "If the investors don't like it, they can have their money back. I'll cover it myself. It's what I should've done from the beginning." Hindsight was twenty-twenty, after all.

"You'll be making a mistake, son," he warned in a chilly voice. "I can't be any part of this."

"I don't remember asking you to." I left him that way, gaping at me from behind his desk. There were things to do, calls to make. There had to be a digital copy of Summer's rough cut backed up somewhere. I'd find it or die trying.

Dad wanted me to take over the studio. It was time for my first official duty—restoring the original film somehow.

Then, I'd spend the rest of my life making this up to the woman who directed it.

If she let me.

20

SUMMER

It took an entire month to prepare for this, practicing my fake smile. To come up with a few ways of deflecting perfectly reasonable questions I would never be able to answer. The sort of stuff people always asked on red carpets. What did this project mean to you? What was your favorite aspect of the experience?

Claudia was my rock through all of it. She stood with me beside the car, which the studio had sent to the hotel to pick us up. At least they were holding up their end of the bargain when it came to accommodations. Any planning had gone through her since she knew there was no way I could handle it.

I was barely handling it now after weeks of psyching myself up, including weeks of ignoring

Lex's attempts at communicating. All I had to do was get through this. I could go back to licking my wounds in San Francisco while struggling to figure out what came next.

"I don't think I can do this," I whispered, eyeing the crowd. How was I supposed to string a few words together for reporters when I could barely breathe? I looked down, ready to see my heart burst out of my chest and all over the simple, sleeveless black Gucci that Claudia had forced me into buying for the occasion. She'd battled me on a lot of things, but there was no getting around my color choice. Black seemed the most logical option.

"You can," she reminded me in a fierce whisper, gripping my hands tight. "And you will. Get your ass in there, show them they haven't beaten you."

That was the problem. They had. They had beaten my dreams out of me, which was even worse. Eric had started it, but Lex and those brainless ass-kissers at the studio had delivered the death blow.

Going through it was one thing, but letting them see it was something else. I called on my breathing, focusing only on it for a few moments. The least I could do was control my nervous system. "Okay," I whispered, giving her a nod. "Let's do it."

"Attagirl. I'm right here with you." But she dropped a step behind, anyway, letting me take the lead. The red carpet stretched out in front of me, chock full of people jockeying to have their faces captured on camera when all I wanted to do was hide.

It was surreal the number of people unrelated to the project who had come out tonight. I recognized one famous face after another. They were here for my movie. What a shame it wouldn't be *my* movie they watched.

I didn't have it in me to read the preliminary, spoiler-free reviews. It hurt too damn much. Now, walking the carpet with my best friend at my back, I wished I had at least skimmed them if only to get an idea of what the general consensus happened to be. Claudia swore up and down people liked it. I couldn't see how.

There was one major blessing on the way into the theater. Nobody recognized me. They might by the time the movie was over, if I were given any recognition after the screening, but I was prepared to run if I had to. Lex could deal with the fallout of his director fleeing the event. After everything he had put me through, he deserved it.

"Oh, fuck me," Claudia muttered, touching my

elbow. I slowed down, turning my head so she could murmur in my ear. "Eric is here. Ten o'clock."

I looked in that direction, and sure enough, there he was, speaking to a reporter who'd shoved a microphone in his face. His golden hair gleamed, his smile was blinding. He had gotten veneers that looked ridiculous like a set of shiny, white horse teeth awkwardly crammed into a hamster's mouth.

"I need to get inside." It was my sole mission now to keep my head down, stay unnoticed, and sidestep the cluster of people around Danica as she was photographed and interviewed near the entrance. She looked stunning and was clearly soaking up the attention.

Did she care that the best part of her performance had been cut from the film? I ached for her and everybody else and wanted so much to apologize or at least make sure they knew it wasn't my fault. I had done my best.

It was a small miracle that I was able to sneak into the theater, dashing straight to the restroom to calm myself. I was shaking, dizzy, and almost tripped and fell in my haste but caught myself in time. Dampening paper towels with cold water and touching them to my pulse points helped cool me down before nervous perspiration turned to sweat.

"You're doing great." Claudia pulled out a comb to touch up my hair. A few soft tendrils had fallen free of the knot at the back of my head. I looked like a ghost with only a slash of red over my lips, giving my face any definition.

"This was a huge mistake," I whispered, meeting my best friend's glance in the mirror.

"I don't think so," she whispered, giving me an awkward side hug. She then adjusted her pinned-up curls and checked out the dark blue, full-length Prada she had picked for the occasion. "I think tonight is going to be a good night. I feel it in my bones."

Then she was delusional. Either that, or she was trying way too hard to pick up my spirits.

"All you have to do is sit in the back of the theater, try to keep a pleasant look on your face, and answer questions if anybody stops you. You don't even have to participate in the Q and A." That was one of my hard-and-fast demands, which she had negotiated for me. I would owe her for the rest of my life, end of story. She had come through in ways I couldn't begin to repay her for.

"What about—" I cut myself off before his name fell out of my mouth.

Not that it mattered. He was the elephant in the

room. "You know he's going to be here." With a grimace, she added, "And he has asked about you in his emails. More than once."

"Good for him." The subject of Lex Landry had been off the table at my insistence. I didn't want to hear his name. I didn't want to hear anything about him. It was bad enough that I missed him with every cell of my being. Bad enough, I couldn't close my eyes at night without seeing his face in front of me. I would wake up and swear I caught the whiff of his cologne, that I felt his touch against my skin, lingering, tingling.

But he would be here tonight, along with his wretched father and the entire team of investors. And they'd look me in the eye and try to be buddy-buddy for the sake of the press. And I would have to play along with the charade or risk making myself into a pariah in front of the entire free world.

The door swung open, and a group of women came in, gossiping, making comments about themselves and pretty much everybody else around them. Who wore this, who said what, who looked like shit. We ducked out, cut across the lobby, and side-stepped photographers. All I had to do was get through this.

We were some of the first people in the theater,

but it filled up quickly. Taking a seat this early meant watching people as they walked in. "Oh, there's that guy that owns the hotels and restaurants," Claudia whispered, nodding toward a tall, handsome guy with dark hair and piercing eyes. "Clayton, something. He helped throw the party on the first day of shooting."

"I know who he is," I whispered. He'd let us stay in his hotel before it opened. A full-body shudder ran through me when I recalled standing on the roof, staring down at a city that would never be mine. It had been a nice fantasy while it lasted.

So Lex had invited his friends. How nice for him. How nice for Eric, who walked in with that bastard, Clyde Harris. They didn't see me, too busy waving and shaking hands. I even recognized a couple of the investors who watched the finished movie with us.

"There he is." Claudia covered a hand over my cold and clammy hand. She was kind and didn't remark on it while staring down at the stage in front of the screen where Lex stepped out.

A wave of red-hot emotion swept over me and left me biting my tongue hard to hold back a cry of pure longing. Oh God, I loved him. I still loved him. I couldn't lie to myself anymore. Setting eyes on him was all it took to know for sure that I'd never, ever get over that man. What we found together, what I thought I found with him, made what I thought I had with Eric look like child's play. Compared to Lex, Eric was a child.

But it wasn't right. It was not meant to be. I would have to continue watching him from a distance. He was the epitome of casual cool, wearing a dark tailored suit with no tie, the top two buttons popped.

Was he wearing that cologne I loved?

"Ladies and gentlemen." His rich voice rang out as he worked the microphone out of its stand. "Thank you so much for being here tonight."

The energy in the room practically crackled as the last few stragglers took their seats. I focused harder on my breathing, keeping myself calm.

Lex smiled in the light of so many beams trained on him. Claudia gave me the gossip about Alexander naming his son as head of the studio. Yet one more thing Lex had lied about—all of his posturing and bullshit. All it took was Daddy handing him the key for him to forget everything he told me about what he really wanted to do with his life. What really mattered.

Once the room went close to silent, he contin-ued, "What you're about to see tonight represents my first executive producer credit. I can't tell you what a gratifying journey this has been." Warm, gentle applause rose while I fought back the bile rising in my throat. The pretentious prick. It was very grati-fying for him, wasn't it? I had made it too easy.

"You're about to see something else, as well." Some of the sunshine drained from his voice. Was I the only one who noticed how serious he got all of a sudden? "This film represents passion. Dedication. Single-minded focus. It was directed by a young woman whose artistic vision is uncompromising. Unflinching. And you'll see the results of that in the completed director's cut we're about to screen for you this evening."

"Director's cut?" I whispered while the same question echoed with confusion behind the looks and whispers flying around.

"All I ask is that you have a little faith." His gaze swept the auditorium like he was looking for some-thing. *Someone.* "And that you understand this was a labor of love."

I couldn't. It was too much, too confusing, too conflicting. Everything in me screamed at me to bolt, so I planted my feet, ready to jump out of my seat and run all the way back to San Francisco if I had to.

"Nope." Claudia's hand was a claw around my wrist, holding me in place. "Sit your ass down and watch."

If anything, I was too stunned to move. "What is happening right now?" I hissed as the lights went down and the screen went bright. She wouldn't answer, but she wouldn't let go, either. She turned her face toward the screen the way everybody else did.

I couldn't hold back the tears that filled my eyes as the first shot appeared on the screen. As the credits began to roll, we watched Danica go through the motions of her morning in the apartment above the garage where she worked. Her grim, tiny apartment was actually a set on the soundstage across from my old office.

I was too busy feeling overwhelmed to realize the obvious. It took a minute or two of me being pulled back and forth between heartache and embarrassment to realize what I was watching.

"My movie." I earned a few curious looks from the people around us, but who cared? It was impossible, but it was true. I turned to Claudia and whispered, "My movie. This is my movie!"

"No shit, Sherlock." Her eyes sparkled with unshed tears. "Watch it. Enjoy it. You deserve it."

My movie.

But how? How did he do it without me knowing? And how the hell did he get away with it? I looked around, convinced everybody was in on it but me. All I saw were people watching a movie, sinking into the world I created.

My world.

And now I was glad I sat in the back so I could watch everybody react. They laughed at the right times and cried a little during the dark moments. I soaked it up like a sponge, still dazed, unable to believe it was happening. It was real. Somehow, Lex had found a way to screen my movie instead of the monstrosity someone tried to turn it into.

When it was over, when the crowd got to their feet and cheered, they weren't cheering for Danica winning the big race.

"Stand up!" Claudia was weeping as she pulled me to my feet and waved an arm overhead. Lex stepped up to the microphone and found me after shading his eyes with one hand.

"Ladies and gentlemen, the director, Summer Strawbridge!" Lex pointed straight at me, and all at once, the lights swung my way, blinding me while the applause swelled. I didn't know where to look, what to do, how to feel. It was a dream come true.

"It was all him!" Claudia shouted, wildly applauding. "He made it happen! He made me swear not to tell you!"

I would kill him. I might kiss him to death, but at the end of the day, he would be dead.

This was everything I'd ever dreamed of—being swarmed, mobbed, congratulated after being swept up in the crowd and practically carried out to the lobby. I probably looked like hell after bawling my eyes out, but that didn't stop the photographers and the journalists from peppering me with questions and shouting their praise.

"Look who it is!" A group of surprise guests cut through the wall of journalists, and suddenly, I was caught up in Mom's embrace. My sisters and dad were there as well. I had made them swear not to come, expecting to be humiliated, but somebody had gone behind my back. He had gone behind my back on a lot of things. I couldn't bring myself to be upset when having them with me made everything perfect.

"It was beautiful. I'm so proud of you!" Mom was more of a mess than I was. "We didn't know anything about this until yesterday after you had already flown out here. He sent a jet and everything!"

I didn't have to ask who she meant. Not when I found Lex watching us, ignoring the reporters asking him questions. I had seen it in movies dozens of times, the rest of the room going blurry and foggy as the two leads locked eyes.

I didn't know it happened in real life.

I didn't know any of this was the sort of thing that happened in real life.

What was there to say? A million questions, of course. A million thanks. A million kicks in his shins for making me think he was dragging me down here to rub my nose in my biggest failure.

"Summer?"

Before I could snap myself out of the hold Lex's gaze had over me, I found his father standing behind me. He extended a hand, wearing a smile that to the rest of the world might look triumphant, but to me appeared... apologetic? Something close to it?

"I don't say this very often," he offered. "But I was wrong. You were right. Can you forgive a stupid old man?"

I knew how much it must've taken for him to put that together and in public. Rumor had it he was going through some health issues. I might have avoided the topic of Lex, but that didn't mean my head was so deep in the sand I didn't notice anything else going on.

Taking his hand, I nodded while flashes went off all around us. "Of course. Thank you for saying that."

"I can honestly say I have hope for the direction this studio will go in." Looking around, he sighed. "New investors, for one thing. New blood."

At my arched eyebrow, he explained, "When the former investors wanted their money back after Lex announced he would release your version, Lex and his friends put up the cash."

Now I understood why Lex's friend was there. They wanted to see what their money went to. "This is all a lot," I admitted, overwhelmed.

"No doubt." His attention shifted to something over my shoulder, and a corner of his mouth pulled upward. "I'll let my son explain the rest."

He was behind me. Somehow, even in the middle of so many people, I could identify Lex's cologne. My heart sang before I turned to find him there, looking contrite. Handsome and contrite. "Surprise?" he murmured.

Throwing myself into his arms would be a mistake. I couldn't make it that easy. "You kept this a secret all this time, and all you have to say to me is surprise?" I asked.

"How about I love you?" he asked, keeping his voice low. "Is that better?"

My heart couldn't take much more of this. Everything I wanted, everything I had missed these past lonely, miserable weeks was now in front of me. Mine for the taking.

Instead of bursting into tears, I replied, "It's a start." I had told myself over and over to forget him, that I was fine without him, better off alone. Funny how all of that evaporated now that he was in front of me, and I knew he had saved the movie and my dream. He protected my dream.

"Whatever it takes, Summer. Everything I have. Everything I'll ever have. All of me." His warm, dark eyes cut from one side to the other. "I'll even throw myself on your mercy in front of half the world. What can I do to make you forgive me?"

I was still frozen by indecision when someone tapped me on the shoulder from behind. "I'll keep the family entertained," Claudia whispered close to my ear. "You two can catch up."

That was exactly what I needed to hear. I threw her a silent, grateful look. We would have words later about her keeping secrets, but for now, I was too busy basking in the joy of the moment. "Why don't we get out of here to discuss this in private?" I suggested.

It probably looked suspicious, the two of us leaving, but I couldn't bring myself to care. I was too busy feeling almost delirious. Could this be real? Was this my life?

Before we could escape, however, the last person I ever wanted to see barged through the crowd, brimming over with false cheerfulness. The man was as transparent as cellophane. "Well, well, well," Eric crowed, all smiles and empty laughter. "I taught you everything you know. Where's my thanks?"

Incredible how many things could go through a person's mind in the blink of an eye. How many ugly, hate-filled thoughts. How much emotion—outrage, disgust, disappointment. All of it and more, raced through me and heated my blood until it boiled.

My mouth opened in preparation to vent every last thought. But it was Lex who spoke. "Your thanks must be somewhere with the invitation you never received," he replied in a clipped, professional tone. Raising a hand, he signaled one of the security guards standing nearby. "We'll take care of that right now by having you escorted off the premises."

Two burly men dressed in black took hold of him. "Hey, wait a minute..."

Just when I thought the night couldn't get any better. I had the pleasure of watching Eric removed from the building, red-faced and quietly protesting, before Lex led me out by the hand and helped me into his waiting limo.

The second we were alone, I turned to him with questions brimming over. "How—" I blurted out, but he cut me off with a deep, searching kiss, my face in his hands, his body pressed close to mine. I had never wanted anything more, but I couldn't let it be so simple. There was still part of me that wouldn't give up.

"Wait." With my hands against his shoulders, I pushed him back, shaking my head when he leaned in for another kiss. "We're skipping over something important."

"I did try to contact you these past few weeks." His ravenous gaze traveled over my face. "I would've told you. Claudia wanted to, but I thought it should come from me."

"All you had to do was tell me—"

He shook his head, touching his fingers to my lips. "Enough fighting, arguing over who should've done what. This was my gift to you and my deep,

deep apology. I should've been fully honest with you from the beginning, but I didn't want to spoil things by telling you there were issues between Dad and me. I thought I could handle them on my own. I was that arrogant. We both were," he concluded with a sigh.

"He told me about your new investors."

"New investors, new everything," he confirmed. "I have you to thank for that. It makes the most sense, but I wouldn't have considered bringing them on if it hadn't been for you providing the impetus."

Tracing the outline of my mouth with his thumb, he whispered, "I've missed you. It was like living the past month with part of me missing. You'll never know the torment."

"I don't think I would go that far." I closed a hand over his, then took a deep breath. Time to be brave and take the first step into the future. "I've missed you too. And what happened back there..."

"Are you happy?" he asked, tender, sweet. "That's all I need to know."

Was I happy? That was a no-brainer. "Why don't you raise that privacy divider?" I whispered, eyeing the front seat. "And we can talk about that."

I didn't have to tell him twice. He leaned over and pressed the button, raising the tinted glass. That and the tinted windows meant no one could see me hiking my dress up around my hips to straddle Lex's lap.

"I guess this means you're forgiven," I announced, kissing him as hard as possible, with every moment of longing, aching, and missing him behind it. I poured it all into him, emptying myself to make room for what came next.

"I love you." He skimmed my neck with his lips, leaving fire in his wake while running his hands up my legs. "I love you so much."

"I love you too." With my arms around his neck, I held him close enough to feel his heart pounding like mine did.

"You know this is just the beginning." His hands moved while he whispered, sliding up under my dress, cupping my ass, and making me moan with my face pressed to his neck. "Now the world knows your name. Nothing is going to stop you."

"Us." Lifting my head, I kissed him gently before staring into his dark eyes. How did I think I could spend the rest of my life without doing this again? "Nothing is going to stop us."

And then I was swept up again, lost in his kiss, his touch, and the thrill of grinding in his lap while riding down the brightly lit streets of Hollywood.

"I need you." He probed greedily at my pussy, working his fingers under my thong, his lips and his tongue lavishing long, searing kisses over my chest. When I pulled down the top of the dress, he eagerly lapped at my nipples, taking me close to the edge after so many long, lonely nights denying myself what I craved most.

I reached between us to unzip him with a trembling hand. "Fuck, yes," he groaned out against my skin. He fumbled in his back pocket with his free hand while I withdrew his thick, rigid length from his pants.

"What do you want me to do with this?" I whispered, lost in lust and the thrill of coming home. Where I belonged. Nothing in San Francisco felt right, but this? This was meant to be. This was forever.

"I want you to ride it," he growled out, unrolling a condom before pulling me back into his lap. "I want inside you. That's the only place I ever want to be. I love you, Summer."

I paused with him at my entrance, staring down at him, wanting to hold this moment for as long as I could. We were taking the first steps down a new road together. This was it.

"I love you." I sank down, taking him inside me,

both of us gasping as our bodies reconnected for the first of many times to come. It took nothing to set me off, and before I knew it, I was shuddering, clinging to him, and moaning his name, riding him for all I was worth.

Claiming him. Claiming us as we cruised down Sunset Boulevard with the world at our feet and nothing but the entire future ahead.

EPILOGUE
TRAVIS

Years from now, if anyone asked me to describe the most hectic, balls-to-the-wall, insane day of my life, I would tell them about today. Sitting at my desk, I wondered how the hell so many things could go wrong in a handful of hours.

It started with being rear-ended on Wilshire Boulevard. The guy behind me thought I was waiting too long to make a left turn, it seemed. It was irritating enough to throw off my morning schedule, but nothing major.

Then came the call from my office manager just as I reached the office, telling me she found a small deluge raining down on the accounts receivable, accounts payable, and payroll departments when she arrived this morning. The burst pipe meant all of the electronics in that area would have to be replaced, and the employees sitting at those desks moved elsewhere for the time being. The constant hum of equipment as the maintenance crew cleaned up the mess had my head aching way too damn early.

But the cherry on top of the shit sundae was the sudden appearance of my four-year-old daughter minutes before I was due to leave for a lunch meeting. "I am so sorry, Mr. Knight," her nanny had babbled, flustered and breathless. "But my agent got me an audition in twenty minutes, and I have to be there. I can't pass it up."

I hoped for her sake the audition went well because she wouldn't work for me another day. After I'd fired her, I had my assistant rearrange my schedule while I called my friend, Spencer. "*What's the name of the agency where you found that part-time girl for Hannah?*" I'd asked, referring to the ten-year-old daughter he shared with his girlfriend, Rowan.

The two of them were devoted parents, but they also had busy careers. The last time they traveled to New York for business, Rowan's parents were both down with the flu, meaning they had to take the kid with them. Rowan had raved about the nanny they found to cover for them while they were in meetings. I had hope there might actually be a few good ones out there.

He'd texted me the information, and I called immediately. After briefly describing my situation to the agency's owner, I explained, "I need someone dependable. I've been burned by three different girls over the last six months. They tell me they're in this for the long haul. Then they drop my daughter as soon as something flashier comes along. I can't afford for this to keep going on."

"Mr. Knight, we cater exclusively to parents in your position." She'd promised she would send someone to interview in my office within an hour.

And she had. She had sent me someone who looked like a character from a children's cartoon show. Sitting behind my desk, from which I ran a shipping empire spanning half the globe, I took in the unusual sight of the young woman before me— blonde pigtails, a floral-print sundress, and a pink backpack over her slim shoulders. She could've passed for a high schooler, though the information the agency had emailed told me she was twenty-four and a recent grad school graduate.

Her sapphire blue eyes sparkled as she extended a hand across the desk. "Mr. Knight?" she asked in an excruciatingly sunny voice, just slightly more painful than stepping on a Lego in bare feet. "I'm Penny Harmon. Your new nanny."

That's what she thought.

NEED MORE?

Dive into this scorching bonus scene from *Broken Rules* here:

https://BookHip.com/PMHNWPB

Enjoy x

RELUCTANTLY YOURS
ELITE MEN OF LOS ANGELES BOOK 3

He's all rules and order, I'm all chaos and color—too bad chemistry doesn't follow the rules.

Travis

I'm used to running an empire, not running after a nanny who looks like a walking rainbow and disrupts my meticulously planned world.

Penny Anderson isn't just unsuitable—she's chaos in pigtails and glitter.

But my daughter adores her, and Penny's sunshine personality slowly chips away at the walls I've built.

She's hiding something behind that unrelenting cheer, and I guess we're similar like that. Still, I shouldn't care. All I should care about is my one rule —don't cross the line.

Too bad she's standing right on it, tempting me every single day.

Penny

Taking a nanny job for a powerful, brooding single dad wasn't supposed to turn my life upside down.

Travis Knight is every bit the cold, calculating CEO —until he's with his daughter, and I catch glimpses of the man behind the mask.

But this job isn't just about Sofia—it's a fresh start I desperately need. If only I could ignore the heat in Travis's eyes and the way he makes me question every rule I've ever set for myself.

....

Available from all good bookstores and my website:

https://authormissywalker.com/collections/elite-men-of-los-angeles

ACKNOWLEDGMENTS

Writing may seem like a solo job, but I have a whole team of incredible people behind me, and I couldn't do this without them.

First, a huge thank you to my dear friend and cleaner, Claudette—I'm so lucky to have you in my life. It's not just about keeping my home in order while my head's off wandering through fictional worlds—it's the kindness, the chats, and the laughter along the way. I don't take you for granted for a second. You mean more to me than you know.

To my family—my husband and my kids—thank you for understanding that sometimes "Mummy's working" means late nights, tight deadlines, and moments when I'm pulled in a million directions. Your patience and support allow me to chase this dream, and I love you for it.

A huge thank you to my incredible beta team— Saskia, you're a force of nature, always pushing me to do better. Karmin, your sharp insights keep me on track. And Clara, your thoughtful feedback brings a fresh perspective every time—I appreciate you all more than words can say.

To the dream team behind the scenes— Lauren and Ella—you make the chaos look effortless, keeping everything running so I can focus on the words. I truly couldn't do this without you both. You're the magic that holds it all together.

If you're looking for a place to laugh, chat, and embrace all things books (with a side of smutty fun), come join us in *Missy Walker's Book Babes* on Facebook. It's a wild, supportive community where we lift each other up and have a damn good time doing it.

Stay fabulous.

Missy x

JOIN MISSY'S CLUB

Hear about exclusive book releases, teasers, discounts and book bundles before anyone else.

Sign up to Missy's newsletter here:
www.authormissywalker.com

Become part of Missy's Facebook Reader Group where we chat all things books, releases and of course fun giveaways!

https://www.facebook.com/groups/
missywalkersbookbabes

ABOUT THE AUTHOR

Missy is an Australian author who writes kissing books with equal parts angst and steam. Stories about billionaires, forbidden romance, and second chances roll around in her mind probably more than they ought to.

When she's not writing, she's taking care of her two daughters and doting husband and conjuring up her next saucy plot.

Inspired by the acreage she lives on, Missy regularly distracts herself by visiting her orchard, baking naughty but delicious foods, and socialising with her girl squad.

Then there's her overweight cat—Charlie, chickens, and border collie dog—Benji if she needed another excuse to pass the time.

If you like Missy Walker's books, consider leaving a review and following her here:

instagram.com/missywalkerauthor
facebook.com/AuthorMissyWalker
tiktok.com/@authormissywalker
bookbub.com/profile/missy-walker

ALSO BY MISSY WALKER

ELITE MEN OF LOS ANGELES

Scarred Heart

Broken Rules

Reluctantly Yours

Entangled Vow

Velvet Sin

Boundless Love

ELITE MEN OF MANHATTAN

Forbidden Lust*

Forbidden Love*

Lost Love

Missing Love

Guarded Love

Infinite Love Novella

ELITE HEIRS OF MANHATTAN

Seductive Hearts

Sweet Surrender

Sinful Desires

Silent Cravings

Sensual Games

Endless Love

ELITE MAFIA OF NEW YORK SERIES

Cruel Lust*

Stolen Love

Finding Love

SLATER SIBLINGS SERIES

Hungry Heart

Chained Heart

Iron Heart

SMALL TOWN DESIRES SERIES

Trusting the Rockstar

Trusting the Ex

Trusting the Player

*Forbidden Lust/Love are a duet and to be read in order.

*Cruel Lust is a trilogy and to be read in order

All other books are stand alones.

www.ingramcontent.com/pod-product-compliance
Lightning Source LLC
Chambersburg PA
CBHW030557170726
48283CB00002B/370